New TOEIC Listening Script

先想文章可能會有的人事時地物·人多還是人少
另外是室外還是室內·空曠還是擁擠
圖片中人的動作是什麼·全部聽完再選答案

texture
n. 織法, 質地
soft }
rough } textured

PART 1

棒球體育場 arena n. 競技場

1. (C) (A) This is a baseball stadium. 泡/
   (B) This is a <u>textile</u> factory. 是間紡織場 /'tekstaɪl/
       textile adj. 紡織的
   (C) This is a swimming pool.
   (D) This is an ice-skating <u>rink</u>. 溜冰場

街頭小販 ; peddler 叫賣小販

2. (A) (A) She is a street <u>vendor</u>. 賣家 = *seller*   *hawker*
   (B) She is a police officer.   *dealer*   *cheap-jack*
   (C) She is a teacher.   *trader*   *monger*
   (D) She is a <u>clerk</u>. 櫃枱人員   *merchant*   *huckste*
       職員·銷售員   *retailer*   *merchandiser*

靠近樹

3. (C) (A) The girl is near the tree.   幾隻鳥在水中   *aquatic adj 水生的*
   (B) Several birds are in the water.   *aquatic plants*
   (C) The girl is wearing a coat. 穿了件大衣
   (D) This is an <u>aquarium</u>. 水族館   Aquarius 水瓶座
       water place   'aquaplane n. 滑水板
                      'ɑːə e

fighting game 格鬥遊戲

4. (A) (A) They are <u>fighting</u>. 打架   *sew*
   (B) They are <u>sewing</u>. 縫紉   /so/ v. 縫紉
   (C) They are dancing. 跳舞   Sewer = tailor
   (D) They are <u>farming</u>. 種植作物   sewing machine

                                    sewage
                                    /'sjuɪdʒ/ n. 汙水
                                    汙穢物

辦公大樓

5. (D) (A) This is an office building.
   (B) This is a public park. 公園
   (C) This is a shopping mall. 商場
   (D) This is a <u>private</u> home. 私人住宅   *private adj.*

做木工   ①個人的 = individual
                  私人的   personal

6. (C) (A) They are <u>woodworking</u>.
   (B) They are <u>cooking</u>. 做飯
   (C) They are <u>landscaping</u>.   ②私密的 = unofficial
   (D) They are <u>painting</u>. 庭園造景   confidential

塗油漆·畫畫
paint n. 顏料·油漆 v. 塗顏色·畫 I'm painting the walls in pink.

GO ON TO THE NEXT PAGE.

U0084652

PART 2

誰做決定把這個活動取消了?

7. (A) Who <u>made the decision</u> to cancel the <u>program?</u> n. 課程、節目、活動、6億、程式
   (A) Not me. 不是我
   (B) That was my favorite program. 那是我最喜歡的活動
   (C) <u>Make the decision.</u> 做決定! You call the shot! 你決定
   You make the call. 你做決定吧! It's your call! 你說了算

8. (C) Do you mind if I sit here? 你介意我生在這兒嗎?
   (A) It's <u>self-serving.</u> → 是自助式的   * improve
   (B) New and <u>improved.</u> → 新的而且改量過的   = better = ameliorate
   (C) <u>I don't mind at all.</u>   ɪ ɪze
   我一點都不介意 not at all 一點都不   → I want to improve all aspects
                                        of my life physically, spiritually
9. (B) Did you make it <u>in time</u> to see James?   and academically.
   (A) It was exciting. 很興奮   你有來得及
   (B) No, I just <u>missed</u> him.   * paint
   (C) On Tuesday. 週二 我剛錯過他 去看James嗎? n. 油漆、顏料
   *miss v 錯過、想念、遺失 You missed my meaning. 你沒有領會我的 v. 畫、塗油漆   (adj)
10. (A) What's wrong with Vincent? Vincent怎麼了? 意思   * be allergic to
   (A) He <u>lost his job</u> today. 他今天失業了
   (B) Paint.   ① 對~過敏
   (C) Don't bring me flowers. <u>I'm allergic.</u> 不要帶花給我, 我過敏
in time / on time. 準時. in time更準   ② 討厭
11. (C) Try to be <u>on time</u> from now on, OK? 從現在開始, 記得要準時 的是嗎?
   (A) What time? How about six? 幾點? 10點如何?
   (B) That's right. He's the boss. 沒錯, 他是老大(老闆)   allergy ⓝ
   (C) I'm sorry. It will never happen again.   ˈælɪdʒɪ 過敏症
                                                          厭惡、反感
12. (A) Can I ask you a question? 可以問你一個問題嗎?
   (A) Of course. 當然可以   to have an allergy to sth.
   (B) It's not my question. 這不是我的問題
   (C) The <u>jury</u> is out. = the jury is still out = a decision has not yet been made.
   n. 陪審團   還沒做出最後決定
13. (B) Will Mary have the TPS reports (by) Monday? Mary可以在周一之前把TPS報告弄好嗎
   (A) The TPS reports.
   (B) She said she would. 他說他會   bypass n. 旁邊的路 v. 繞道
   (C) See you on Monday. 周一見囉 bystander n. 旁觀者 / by product 副產品
                                                   by-election notice 補選告
14. (C) What time does your flight leave? 你的飛機何時離開?
   (A) Leave it up to me. 讓我來決定吧 leave it up to sb. 讓某人決定
   (B) <u>Boom</u> goes the dynamite.
   (C) Noon. 轟到我了(感到意外) * dynamite
   → 雷、大炮、隆聲   n. 炸藥、驚人的人、物

48

15. (C) Do you have any plans this weekend? 這周末你有任何計畫嗎?
    (A) Michigan. 密西根
    (B) We get paid by the hour. 我們按小時收薪水 　　＊搭帳篷‧扎營
    (C) I'm going camping with some friends. 和一些朋友去露營　set up the tent
Camp n. 營地‧帳篷 v. 紮營 Where shall we camp tonight? 　　　　set up a camp

16. (C) Did John make a speech at the meeting? John在會議中有演講嗎?
    (A) Everyone was talking at once. 大家都同時說話 at once = at the same time
    (B) There were five people. 有5個人
    (C) No, Steve did all the talking. Steve負責所有的發言　　＊ record
talking book 有聲書‧ talking point 話題‧論據　　　　/ rɪ'kɔrd / (v)
17. (B) I think we're lost. 我想我們迷路了　　　　　　記載‧記錄
    (A) We have a winning record. 我們有得獎‧紀錄　/'rekəd / (n)
    (B) Let's ask someone for directions. 我們來問問別人方向　記錄‧唱片‧成績‧前科
    (C) Alas, poor Yorick.　　　　It's an all-time record.
    嘆 喉,可憐的 Yorick　　　　　　　歷史最佳成績
18. (B) Why did you get fired from your job? 你為何被解雇
    (A) I got fired yesterday. 我昨天被解雇 解雇　He has no record. 無前科
    (B) It's a long story. 說來話長　　　a clean record. 無前科
    (C) I'm doing the work of two people. 我一個人做2個人的工作
你有找到人替代Martha嗎?
19. (B) Have you found a replacement for Martha?　→ You won't like it.
    (A) He was a man of infinite jest. 他是個充滿笑點的人 + Let me make it short.
    (B) Not yet. 還沒有
    (C) Martha is leaving. Martha要離開了 ＊replacement ＊infinite　jest
    你昨晚和Henry的約會如何? n.代替‧代替(物)/人 adj.無限的 毛ɪ笑
20. (A) How was your date with Henry last night? + cost 更替費用 極大的 笑柄
    (A) It was nice. 很不錯　　　+staff 更替人員 make a jest of sb.
    (B) I saw Henry last night. 我昨晚看到他 ＊guarantee make fun of sb.
    (C) It's the tenth. 是第10次 n.保證‧(書)‧擔保
    你有健康保險,對吧! v.保證: The policy guarantees us
21. (C) You have health insurance, don't you?　against all loss.
    (A) How about if I guarantee it? 如果我保證可以嗎? 保障免受任何損失
    (B) Crumbs. 碎屑　＊a crumb of　A few crumbs of praise for
    (C) No, I can't afford it. 少許～　their hard work.
    不,我付不起
22. (A) Where can I find a stapler? 哪裡可以找到釘書機? → staple n.釘書針
    (A) Look in the supply cabinet. 看侯應櫃 (放備用文具的櫃子)
    (B) Put the stapler on my desk. 放我桌上
    (C) I stapled them together. 把他們釘在一起
    staple v. 釘在一起
Staple adj. 主要的 → Rice is our staple food. 天氣構成他們談話的主內容

GO ON TO THE NEXT PAGE.
n. 釘書針‧主題‧主張. The weather forms the staple of their conversation.

23. (C) That's Mr. Brown's car, isn't it? 那是布朗先生的車是吧? *ski run 滑雪道.坡
    (A) Oh, I don't drive. 我不開車   ski jump 跳台滑雪
    (B) Mr. Brown.   ski plane 雪上飛機
    (C) No, that's a Lexus. Mr. Brown drives a BMW.

你知道如何滑雪嗎? *ski 滑雪 → a ski suit 滑雪衣
24. (B) Do you know how to ski? n.滑雪板 cross-country skis 越野滑雪板
    (A) I don't have a dog.
    (B) No, I've never been skiing. 我從來沒有滑過 *hang n.做法.用法
    (C) Yes, you will get the hang of it. 你會抓到訣竅 v.懸掛.垂下.逗留

你開始寫提案了嗎? =plan → Her hair hung down on her shoulders.
25. (C) Have you started writing the proposal? → I hung about for an hour,
    (A) The job starts tomorrow.   but he didn't come.
be able to 能夠
    (B) No, I wasn't able to take it. 我不能拿.不能接受 → propose v.提議
    (C) Yes, it will be finished this afternoon. prose n.散文

I want to sit in (the) front of the car. 內部的前面 今天下午會結束
26. (A) Why are there police in front of the building? 外部的前面 無聊的演講
    (A) Someone must have called them. 一定有人打給他們 → He delivered a long prose.
    (B) More often than not. 大多數的時候 More often than not Tom studies English
    (C) Four, counting me. 加上我.四個 during his spare time.

不要再吼了,我就坐在這兒 他常利用業餘時間學英語
27. (A) Stop shouting. I'm sitting right here.
    (A) Sorry, I'll try to keep my voice down. 不好意思,我會保持聲音低一點
    (B) Sit by the window. 坐在窗戶邊
    (C) The man shouted at me. 這男的對我大吼 *shout
    v.喊叫 n.喊叫

28. (C) How long did it take you to get here? 花了你多少時間才到這兒 a shout of protest
    (A) It should be here soon. 應該馬上就到了 a shout of excitement
    (B) I've been here since Monday. 我從周一就在這兒了 → There is nothing much to
    (C) About an hour. 大概一小時 shout about! 用不著那樣嚷嚷

*營業時間
29. (C) What time do you close? 你幾點關門? → People were shouting abuse
    (A) I'm very close with him. office hours 人們在破口大罵
        我和他非常親近 business hours
    (B) No, he didn't. shop hours
    (C) We close at five p.m. 5點關門 bank hours

30. (B) Has today's mail been sent out yet? 今天的信寄出去了嗎? *send out ①.寄出
    (A) Let me think. 讓我想想 ②.打發出去
    (B) Yes, it has. 有啦 → He sent the children out
    (C) It was cancelled. 已被取消了 so that the house might be quiet.

*cancel   This will cancel your debt to me. You should cancel this preposition in the
取消.中止.抵消   這可抵消你欠我的債務   sentence. 你該刪去句子中的介系詞.

31. (B) Are those your shoes?
(A) Adidas.
(B) Yes, they are.
(C) I'm wearing shoes.

*loaf n. 一條或一塊麵包 : a loaf of bread
101
v. 虛度: He loafed away the whole evening.
閒晃: He loafed around for two years.
Don't loaf, please get the job done.
└ =idle =lounge =loiter =lie around

PART 3

<u>Questions 32 through 34</u> refer to the following conversation between three speakers.

M : Excuse me, are you the manager? 打擾一下.你是經理嗎?

Woman UK : Yes. Is there a problem, sir? 是的. 有什麼問題嗎?

我們的特製肉捲 (UP)   我的服務生 Tiffany 說了好幾次

M : I ordered the <u>meat loaf</u> special. My server Tiffany said it would be <u>out</u> several times, but I'm
obviously still waiting. 您大概較之前下單的   要出菜了, 但我仍然在等.

Woman UK : About how long ago did you place your order, sir?

M : At least 25 minutes. 至少25分鐘   那真是不合理   讓我去看看為何有耽擱問.

n. 用餐的人

Woman UK : Oh, that's <u>unreasonable</u>. Let me find out what <u>the holdup</u> is. Tiffany, this diner has
been waiting nearly half an hour for his meal 這位客人已經等了將近30分鐘了

③②

Woman US : I'm very sorry, Ms. Reagan. I've asked the chef, but the kitchen is really slow
tonight. Two of the line cooks are out sick. Maybe you could step in and make things
happen for this gentleman?

Woman UK : Right. Thanks, Tiffany. Sir, I'll ask the chef to send out your meal right away.
好的. 謝謝了 Tiffany. 我會請主廚馬上送出您的餐點.

32. (D) Who most likely is Ms. Reagan?
(A) A travel agent. 旅專
(B) A bank clerk. 銀行行員
(C) A warehouse supervisor. 倉管
(D) A restaurant manager. 餐廳經理

我已詢問過主廚.但是今晚廚房動作很
慢.有二位專門廚師生病請假
也許你可以介入並讓這位先生的餐點發生
(快點上菜)

在抱怨什麼?

33. (A) What is the man <u>complaining about</u>?
(A) An order has not arrived. 訂餐未到   line cook:專門做某樣菜的廚師
(B) A bill is <u>not accurate</u>. 帳單不正確 = inaccurate =incorrect   accurate adj.
(C) An item has been discontinued. 商品不再發行   正確的 =correct
(D) A <u>reservation</u> was lost. 預訂遺失了 (沒訂到)   精確的 =perfect =exactly
預約.禁獵區.自然保護區

34. (B) What does the manager say she will do? 經理說他會如何處理?
(A) Delete an account. 刪除帳號   * refund v 退還.償還
(B) Speak to an employee. 和員工談談   'refund n. to get a refund
(C) <u>Refund</u> a purchase.   退款金額
(D) <u>Confirm</u> an address. →退貨 *purchase
確認地址   n. 購買(之物)、緊抓   GO ON TO THE NEXT PAGE.
He got a purchase on a branch until we came to his rescue.

51

Questions 35 through 37 *refer to the following conversation.*

*poppy cock 胡說

M : I'll have a bagel with cream cheese and a small iced coffee.

W : What type of bagel would you prefer? We have poppy seed, onion, and plain. ≠tasteless 沒味道的

M : The poppy seed sounds good. And give me extra cream cheese. Oh, but not too much sugar in the coffee.

W : We don't add sugar to your coffee, sir. It's self-serve. You can add sugar at the condiment station to your left.

35. (B) Who are the speakers?
    (A) Teacher and student.
    (B) Employee and customer.
    (C) Doctor and patient.
    (D) Friend and foe.

*foe n. 危害物
The bacco is a foe to health.
enemy   adversary
opponent /ˈædvɚˌsɛri/

36. (B) Where is this conversation most likely taking place?
    (A) In an office.
    (B) In a cafeteria.
    (C) On a bus.
    (D) At a business meeting.

*plain adj.
① 清楚的: The meaning of the sentence is very plain.
② 坦白的/直率的: I must be plain with you.
③ 一般的: He has a plain face.
④ (CD) 完全地: He's just plain stupid.

37. (C) What does the man ask for?
    (A) An onion bagel.
    (B) Extra sugar in the coffee.
    (C) Extra cream cheese on the bagel.
    (D) Hot coffee.

Questions 38 through 40 *refer to the following conversation.*

M : Mary, did you contact technical support about my computer yet? You know I'm working on the Cooper presentation and all my work is on that hard drive.

W : I called them yesterday, Rex. They said they'd have a guy out here tomorrow afternoon.

M : Tomorrow afternoon? Oh, no, no, no, Mary. That's not going to work! I'm meeting with Cooper and his associates at three o'clock tomorrow afternoon. This is our most important account. I need you to get someone out here today—today—no excuses, spare no expense.

W : OK, Rex. I'll try my best.

M : Don't try. Just do it. If the tech support people won't come, call an independent repairman. I don't care who you have to call. I want that computer fixed today.

*present vt. 呈現
present n. 禮物 adj. 現在的
presentable adj. 體面的
present-wit 機智

52

38. (B) What is the man's problem? 有什麼問題   ＊shattered
   confident   (A) His schedule is too full. 行程太滿了   adj. 破碎的
   adj.   (B) His computer isn't working. 電腦壞了   心煩意亂的
   有信心的   (C) His confidence is shattered.   shatter v. 粉碎. 動搖
   確信的→They're confident of success.   他的自信心粉碎了   → Nothing could shatter his faith.
   (D) His secretary is on vacation. 祕書在渡假
39. (B) What will the man do tomorrow at three o'clock?   The glass shattered.
   leave for   (A) Buy a new computer. 買新電腦
   離開某地   (B) Meet with a client. 和客戶見面   ＊ leave A for B
   去某地   (C) Leave for a business trip. 去出差   離開前往B地
   (D) Contact customer service. 和客服聯繫   拋棄某人追求他人
40. (A) What will Mary most likely do next?   → He left his wife for one of his students.
   (A) Find someone to fix Rex's computer. 找人修 Rex 的電腦
   associate   (B) Cancel the meeting with Cooper. 取消和 Cooper 的會議   Automatic
   v. 聯想   (C) Meet with Cooper and his associates. 和 Cooper 及同事見面   Telling
   使有聯繫   (D) Fix Rex's computer herself. 自己去修他的電腦   Machine
   結交. 交往 He associates with all sorts of people. 他與各種各樣的人交往.

Questions 41 through 43 refer to the following conversation.
   很高興見到你   需要你的幫忙   ATM把我的卡吃掉了   { credit card / debit card / cash card

W : Hi, James! I'm so happy to see you. I need your help. The ATM took my debit card. What
   should I do? 我該怎麼做?   是在銀行裡的還是在其他地方?   { 信用卡 / 扣帳卡 / 提款卡

M : Where did it happen? Was it at the bank or somewhere else?
   購物中心裡的 ATM
W : I used an ATM at the shopping mall. 應該要有號碼可以打.來處理這些情況

M : OK, well, there should be a phone number to call for these situations. Let's go and check
   the ATM at the mall. 我們去看看吧   ＊ drive v. 開車. 迫使
   → He drove her to admit it.
W: OK, I'll drive. 我來開車   n. 活動 There is a drive for funds.
   比賽 There is a bridge drive.
41. (D) What is the woman's problem?   動力 He is a man of great drive.
   駕照掉了   (A) She lost her driver's license.   幹勁十足的人
   錢包掉了   (B) She lost her wallet.
   手機掉了   (C) She lost her cell phone.   ＊ license   to license sb. to do sth.
   提款卡掉了   (D) She lost her ATM card.   n. 執照. 許可證↗   許可某人做某事
42. (A) What does the man ask?   v. 批准 Are you licensed to drive? 你有被允許
   (A) Where it happened.   開車嗎?
   (B) How it happened.
   (C) When it happened.   ＊debit card   { withdraw 提
   (D) Why it happened.   credit   deposit 存
＊license 補充例句 (思想言行)自由放縱   cash
We must make a distinguish between
freedom and license.   have an overdraft 透支
自由和放縱要區分開來   be in the red 赤字
   black 有盈餘

GO ON TO THE NEXT PAGE.

43. (B) What will the speakers most likely do next?
*in case
①以防萬一
②假使= In case she comes back, let me know immediately.
→ In case I am prevented from coming, please excuse me.
苟我因故不能前來. 請見諒

pick up the phone
打電話
(A) Make a phone call. 打電話
(B) Drive to the shopping mall.
(C) Walk to the bank.
(D) Try another ATM.
hang up the phone 掛電話

Questions 44 through 46 refer to the following conversation.
hiss at sb. 噓某人 *Charge to v. 突擊. 進攻
又不吃午餐了嗎 Wanda?
M : Skipping lunch again, Wanda? 又(發出 噓聲). 午餐. 那是什麼?
W : (Makes hissing sound) Lunch? What's that?
/hɪs/ 我聽說你老闆在生氣 他讓會計部的每個人都處在高度警戒
M : I heard your boss is on the war path. He's got everybody in accounting on high alert, too.
W : You guys in marketing have no idea what it's like to work for that man. I'm afraid to leave
my desk even to use the bathroom, just in case he comes charging in here looking for God
knows what.
bathroom stool 浴室凳 你們行銷部門的人根本不知道幫那個人工作是什麼樣子. 我很怕離開座位了
44. (B) What are the speakers discussing? 即使只是上廁所. 以防他突擊這裡
discuss(v) → discussion 找些誰知道他要什麼的東西.
(A) Lunch. discuss(v)
(B) The woman's boss.
(C) Former clients. = 前客戶. 顧客 = customer = patron
(D) A shortcut to the cafeteria. 去自助餐館的捷徑
(補充)① in the event 到頭來
→ If you play with fire, 結果 you'll get burnt in the event.
burn — burned — burnt
女生暗指什麼?
45. (C) What does the woman imply?
unable adj.不能的 無能的
(A) She's not hungry. 她不餓
(B) She's already had lunch. 已吃過午餐
(C) She's unable to leave her desk. 無法離開座位
(D) She's happy with her job.
② play sb. along 使人焦急等待
→ Stop playing me along. Tell me what happened.
incapable. incompetent. unqualified
46. (B) Where does the man work?
③ play along with 假意與某人合作, 嗯~的呼嚨
→ she was in charge, so I had to play along with her odd ideas.
(A) In sales. 銷售部門
(B) In marketing. 行銷
(C) In accounting. 會計
(D) In tech support. 技術部
→ I know you don't like Jack's idea, but just play along with him for a while.
玩樂器 Play instruments (n.) 1.樂器 2.儀器
The dentist picked up several instruments.

Questions 47 through 49 refer to the following conversation.
真是場好表演. Norman. 你不在哪裡學的?
W : That was a great performance, Norman. Where did you learn to play like that?
M : Where or when? My family moved around a lot, so it's not like I was ever in one place for
very long. I've been playing since I was four. 何時還是何地? 我又身常搬家. 所以我從沒在一個
地方待非常久. 我從4歲就開始演奏了
W : I mean, did you take lessons or go to a special school?
M : Oh, I see. Neither, actually. I'm completely self-taught. I basically learned by playing along
to the radio. 或. 我聽懂了. 其實. 兩者都沒有. 我完全是自學. 我基本上是跟著收音機彈的
我的意思是. 你有上課或者是去特殊學校嗎?

47. (C) What did Norman do?
(A) He moved around on stage.
(B) He grew up quickly.
(C) He gave a performance.
(D) He left too soon.

48. (A) What does the woman ask?
(A) Where did Norman learn his skill?
(B) Where did Norman grow up?
(C) When did Norman take lessons?
(D) What was Norman's family like?

49. (B) What is implied about Norman?
(A) He's arrogant.
(B) He's a musician.
(C) He's from a foreign country.
(D) He's ashamed of his skill.

Questions 50 through 52 refer to the following conversation with three speakers.

M : Hi, Evelyn. I'd like you to meet our new public relations officer, Caroline Wright.

Woman UK : It's nice to meet you, Caroline. Welcome to the firm.

Woman US : Thanks. It's nice to meet you, too.

M : She'll meet the rest of the PR team later today. But I wanted to introduce you now since I believe you live pretty close to each other. Evelyn, I know you were looking for someone to share rides with.

Woman UK : Yes! Caroline, where do you live?

Woman US : Near Sunset Avenue and Carver Street, in West Palmdale.

Woman UK : Oh! I'm at Hollywood and Carver! That's so close! Would you be interested in carpooling together?

Woman US : Sure! That would be great. Can I get your phone number so that we can discuss it later today?

50. (B) In which department do the speakers work?
(A) Accounting.
(B) Public Relations.
(C) Human Resources.
(D) Marketing.

GO ON TO THE NEXT PAGE.

55

[Handwritten annotations:]
move about 四處走動 到處旅行
* be ashamed of 可恥的, 羞愧 adj.
→ I am ashamed of having failed in the exam. 因考試不及格而覺得慚愧
Do you know where he moves about? 你知道他搬到那裡去了嗎?
他在舞台上走來走去
長大很快
表演、履行、完成
太快離開
* shame n. 羞恥 [e]
羞愧感
如何習得技能
哪裡長大
哪裡上課
→ He felt great shame at having failed the exam.
他家人是怎麼樣的
arrogant = insolent = haughty = too proud = cavalier
n. 令人遺憾的事
performer / instrumentalist / composer / songwriter / conductor / maestro / artist / accompanist 伴奏者、伴唱者
傲慢的, 自大的
音樂家
外國來的
對於他的技能感到羞愧
→ It's a shame I haven't heard from you for years.
* public adj. 公眾的, 公用的
He made the secret public. 公開了這個秘密
我想要你見見我們新的公開人員
歡迎來到我們公司
她今天晚點會和其他公關團隊見面
很高興認識你 →但是我想現在介紹你, 因為
我相信你們住得很近。Eve 我知道你在找人共乘 look for 尋找, 期待
I don't look for much profit from the business.
沒錯. Caroline 你住哪裡
很近! 你有興趣共乘嗎? 我不期待生意有太多的收穫
carpool 共乘
當然! 可以要你的電話號碼. 晚點我們可以討論一下嗎?
* source 消息來自可靠人士
n. 源頭, 來源 The news comes from a reliable source.
* resource n. 資源, 財力, 機智, 娛樂
會計
He is a man of resource. 是個足智多謀的人
公關部 Reading is a great resource. 讀書是一種極好的消遣
人資部 HR The exploitation of natural resources was hampered by the lack of technicians.
行銷
自然資源的開發因缺少技術人員而受阻.

51. (D)　What does Caroline Wright ask for?
　　(A) An instruction manual. 操作指南
　　(B) A password. 密碼
　　(C) Some survey results. 研究結果
　　(D) A telephone number. 電話號碼

*manual n. 手冊　adj. 手的、體力的
hand
guide book　　　manual labor
handbook　　　　體力勞動

→ The story is very well organized.
服務業人員也有權組織工會
/ Service workers also have the right to organize.

52. (B)　What does the man suggest that the women do?
組織、安排 (A) Organize an event. 組織活動
使有條理 (B) Drive to work together. 一起開車去上班
　　(C) Share a workspace. 分享工作空間
　　(D) Submit a resume. 繳交履歷

*resume v. 重新開始
/rɪˈzum/　恢復、收回
→ They won the battle and
resumed lost territory.
打勝仗並收回失地

under | send (n) 繳交履歷 → resume /rɪˈzjum/ 恢復、繼續
　　　　　　　　　　　　重新開始　　resume n. 履歷
　　　　　　　　　　　　　　　　　/rɛzjúme/　摘要

Questions 53 through 55 refer to the following conversation.

W : Did you get my e-mail? 你有沒有收到我的郵件
M : Yes, obviously. That's why I'm here. What did you need to see me about? 你找我有什麼事?
　　當然有啊!　　那正是我在這的原因.
W : Apparently, there's a rumor going around that Ben is going to leave the company. Do you
　　know anything about it? 有謠言說 Ben 要離開公司了, 你知道任何相關的事嗎?
M : This is the first time I'm hearing of it. What makes you think I might have any information?
　　I'm just a lowly mail clerk. 這是我第一次聽到那. 是什麼讓你覺得我可能有任何資訊?
= obviously = clearly　　　　　　　　　　　我只是個低階的郵務人員

53. (A)　What are the speakers discussing?
paparazzi 狗仔
① habit　　(A) Company gossip. 公司八卦
習慣、習性 (B) Study habits. 研讀習慣
Ivy has a　(C) Political theory. 政治理論
climbing habit. 常春藤有向上爬的習性 (D) Vacation time. 放假時間 ②氣質

*lowly adj. 地位低的 ←→ high-ranking
highly adv. 高度地、非常地　　等級高的
　　　　　　　　　　　　　　職位高的
He admires her cheerful habit of mind.
→ pull one's rank on a person
仗勢欺人
Rumor has it that~
有謠言說~

54. (C)　What does the woman ask the man? 是否想離開公司
　　(A) If he plans on leaving the company.
　　(B) If he has spoken to Ben recently. 最近是否有和 Ben 說話
　　(C) If he knows anything about a rumor. 知道謠言的任何內容嗎?
　　(D) If he wants to have lunch. 是否想用午餐

imply　Her silence implied consent.
= suggest　她的沉默意味著同意.
hint

55. (A)　What does the man imply? 暗示啥?
　　(A) He has low status within the company. 他在公司內地位不高
　　(B) He doesn't pay attention to gossip. 他沒注意那些八卦 pay attention to
　　(C) He has a close relationship with Ben. 他和 Ben 很親近 注意、當心、聽從
　　(D) He might be the source of the rumor. 他可能是謠言的來源

→ The news comes from a reliable source.
→ Do you know the source of Amazon River? 根源
→ The library has quantities of reference sources. 有大量可供參考的原始資料

56

Questions 56 through 58 *refer to the following conversation.*

W : Hi. That's my Honda out there. It's, um, making a really strange noise. 我的車發出很奇怪的聲音 n. 聲響、噪音 v. 謠傳 It was noised about that the /nɔɪs/ foreign minister intended

M : Can you describe the noise? Where is the noise coming from? 你可以形容一下這個聲音嗎? 從哪裡來的? grind/graɪnd/磨、磨 to resign.

W : Well, it sounds like metal rubbing on metal, or something grinding against something metal. I think it's coming from the engine. I don't know anything about cars. The noise is really horrible. 聽起來像金屬磨擦金屬, 或是有東西大力. 磨到、並到鐵屬 我覺得是引擎發出的聲音 外界說外交官打算 我不太懂得車了, 但聲音真的很可怕 辭職

M : OK, well, let's have a look under the hood. 好的那~我們來看看引擎底下吧? *hood n. 頭巾、罩子 hoodie n. 帽T

對話在哪裡發生
56. (A) Where is this conversation taking place?
repair (A) At an auto repair shop. 汽車維修店
修補 (B) At a discount grocery. 折扣雜貨店
糾正 (C) At a metal processing factory. 金屬加工
恢復 (D) At a busy intersection. 繁忙的十字路口
It took a long time for him to repair his health.

57. (C) What kind of problem does the woman have?
pilot (A) Auto-immune. disease 自身免疫病 autoimmune adj. 自我免疫的
v. 領航 (B) Auto-pilot. 自動駕駛 Immune adj. 免疫的.
駕駛 (C) Automotive. 汽車的、自動推進的 Immune system 免疫系統
n. 飛行員、領導人 (D) Automatic. 自動的 → The washing machine is fully automatic.

58. (B) What will the speakers most likely do next? 接下來會做什麼?
inspect (A) Sign a contract. 簽合約 {close a deal 完成 交易
v. 檢查 (B) Inspect the woman's car. 檢查車子 make a deal 做 交易
審查 (C) Shake hands and call it a deal. 握手完成交易 *deal 交易、大量
(D) Watch a video about automobile maintenance.
*maintain v. 維持、保持、保養 /ˈmentənəns/ → He had given this question a great deal of thought. 這個問題做過許多思考

Questions 59 through 61 *refer to the following conversation.*

你有聽說Bill要被調到Oslo的總部嗎? =head office =base adj. adv. 獨立一人的地
W : Did you hear that Bill Rubin is being transferred to headquarters in Oslo?

M : Really? That's a shocker. He's been killing it here, especially since he came back from Shanghai with all those Chinese accounts. Did you know he single-handedly doubled our revenue in London? 令人驚訝的消息。他在這裡超強的,尤其自從他帶著那些中國部門從上海回來後接管了。你知道他一個人讓我們的收入翻倍嗎。

W : Well, that's probably why he's taking over for Brent Hines as director of European operations. Their numbers are in the tank. They need a superstar like Rubin to save the sinking ship. 嗯。也許那就是為何他接替Brent做為歐洲營運主管。他們的數字一直下降 他們需要像Rubin一樣的超級明星 來拯救這艘下沈的船

M : Well, good for Bill. But I've got to say, I'd rather go anyplace other than Norway in the dead of winter. 對Bill來說是好事阿! 但我必需說,在這寒冬裡我寧願去任何地方也不要去挪威

in the dead of winter 寒冬
night 深夜

GO ON TO THE NEXT PAGE.

59. (A) Why is Bill Rubin being transferred to Oslo? 為何被轉調到 Oslo

placate
e e
v. 撫慰
和解
懷柔

(A) To become director of European operations. ＊operate 變逐, 營運
(B) To placate Chinese investors. 安慰大陸的投資者　操作, 起作用
(C) To increase sales in London. 增加倫敦的銷售 → The medicine operated quickly.
(D) To assist Brent Hines. 協助 Brent → The machine is not operating properly.

60. (B) Where did Bill Rubin double revenues? 他在何處讓營收翻兩倍?

assist
v. 幫助
— 出席

(A) Shanghai. ＊fit
(B) London. v. ①合身 This jacket doesn't fit me.　adj. 健康的
(C) Oslo. ②適合於: Her training fits her for the job.　能勝任的
(D) Paris. ③安裝: Can you fit the electric fire for me?　合適的

61. (A) What does the man imply? 他暗指什麼?　He is not fit to be a lawyer.
You look very fit, Tony.

不知什麼原因
不肯出席
招待會

(A) Norway is extremely cold in winter. 挪威冬天很冷
(B) Shanghai would have been a better fit 上海是個比較適合的地方
(C) London won't miss him. 倫敦不會想念他　(錯過)
(D) Oslo is flooded. 淹到了　n. 適合, 合身

→ She refused to assist at the reception for reasons unknown. The dress is a beautiful fit.

Questions 62 through 64 refer to the following conversation.

我試著要聯繫前台　我要如何轉接你的電話呢?

W : Best Western Gateway, front desk, this is Amy speaking. How may I direct your call?
M : Um, yeah, I was trying to get in touch with the front desk. I'm in room 303...
這裡就是前台　我該如何幫助你呢?
W : Sir, this is the front desk. How can I help you? 有點難為情, 但是我們沒辦法搞懂如何使用電視
M : Oh, right. Well, you see, this is kind of embarrassing but I can't seem to figure out how the
想出, 理解, 明白
television works. I mean, it's on, but all I get is a blank blue screen.
我的意思是, 電視是開的, 但我看到的就是空白的藍色螢幕
W : Room 303? OK, sir. I'll send housekeeping up there right away to resolve your issue. Is
there anything else I can do for you? 我找房務員去解決你的問題, 有任何我可以幫到
resolve → resolution 決心. 決定. 決議　會上　你的地方嗎?

62. (C) Where are the speakers?
(A) In school. 在學校　＊face the issue 面對 問題
(B) On a television set. 電視機裡　raise the issue 提出
(C) In a hotel. 飯店
(D) On a journey. 旅程中　解手. 提出. 加薪. 養育. 募款

to reach the end of one's journey 到車輪盡頭　＊blank adj. 空白的, 茫然的
63. (C) What is the man's problem?　→ There was a blank look
(A) His room is too cold. 房間太冷　on his face.
(B) He would like to order room service. 想叫客房服務　臉上茫然的表情
(C) The television isn't working. 電視壞了
(D) The walls are too thin. 牆太薄 (隔音不好)　v. 消失, 變得模糊
發生故障 out of order
The railway traffic is out of order owing to floods. → The TV screen blanket out.
洪水使鐵路交通中斷

58

64. (B) What does the woman say she will do?

replace (A) Replace the television in the man's room. 重換男生房裡的電視
v. 取代 (B) Send someone to solve the man's problem. 請某人去解決這人的問題
歸還 (C) Reset the cable television system. 重新設定電視系統 (有線電視)
放回原處 (D) Move the man to a different room. 把他搬到不同房間

I'll replace the cup I broke. 我願用一個新杯子賠償我打碎的那個杯子.

Questions 65 through 67 refer to the following conversation with three speakers.

我召集這個會議是要升級公司的"新款智慧型手機找尋餐廳 App"

Woman UK : I've called this meeting to get an update on our company's new restaurant finder
我們等開始消費者測試 下個月
smart phone application. We're due to start consumer testing of the app next month.
優良開發長
Darren, you're the lead developer. Why don't you bring us up to date? 你何不跟我們說說最新
消息

M : Unfortunately, we've had some bugs in the app software. That's why I asked Meredith to
很不幸地 我們App軟體有些問題
join us. She's in charge of software development. 所以我才請 Meredith 加入我們
responsible for 她主要負責軟體開發
通到

Woman UK : Meredith, what can you tell me?

Woman US : Well, we've run into some unexpected problems with a feature that tracks the
這是公司重要的產品 遇到一些非預期中的問題
users' current location. We're hoping to get it fixed shortly. →追蹤使用者目前位置的功能. 希望儘快修好

Woman UK : This is an important product for our company. So, Darren, please send me a
徹底的. 詳盡的
thorough update by the end of the day tomorrow. 請寄給我完善的更新在明天下班前.

M : Absolutely, Ms. Barrymore. As soon as possible. 儘快 before it is too late (在無法挽回以前)
x   o   絕對地=沒問題 ASAP / a.s.a.p   as quickly as possible

65. (A) What are the speakers talking about?
tablet (A) A smart phone application. 智慧型手機App   with all | speed
平板.門牌 (B) Computer tablets. 平板電腦   *mention | haste
匾.碑.藥片 (C) Music players. =walkman 隨身聽 v. 提及. 說起
(D) Digital cameras. 數位相機   mentionable   *estimate
The doctor told me to take two tablets after every meal. adj. 可提到的 v. 估計.估量
66. (D) What problem does the man mention?   值得提到的   n. 估計.估價單
shortage (A) Customer testing has been delayed. 客戶測試被拖延 評斷.看法
缺少.不足 (B) Costs have been higher than estimated. 成本比估計的高
(C) There has been a shortage of parts. 有些部分有缺失   My estimate of
(D) Some software is not working properly. 有些軟體無法運作 the situation is
There is a shortage of salt in this country.
67. (A) What does the man mean by //"Absolutely, Ms. Barrymore."//? not so optimistic.
accept (A) He will provide a report. 會提供報告
接受.承諾 (B) He will hire more programmers. 雇用更多程式設計師
認可.相信 (C) He believes the problem has been resolved. 他相信問題已被解決
(D) He accepts responsibility for the mistake. 他接受這個錯誤的責任
*provide for 提供   他接受這個錯誤的責任
with 供給 She managed to provide   (承擔這個錯誤該負的責任)
her kids with food and clothes.
that 規定 The law provides that these ancient buildings
must be preserved.

GO ON TO THE NEXT PAGE.

你有注意到走廊櫃裡的燈燒掉了嗎?

M : Did you notice the light is <u>burned out</u> in the hallway closet? → *When you burn out, you lose enthusiasm.*

burn out ① 燒盡.斷
② 失去熱情

W : Yes, I did. I was going to ask you to change it.

我有注意到啊:我正要請你去更換

spare { room / cash / time }

備用的燈泡

M : No problem. Do we have any <u>spare bulbs</u>? energy smart

W : We do. <u>I picked up</u> a couple of those new <u>energy-saving</u> bulbs from the <u>hardware store</u>.

= purchased   *我在5金行買了幾個省電的燈泡*

68. (**D**) What does the man ask the woman?

'recognise /ɪɡˈ/
v. 承認
認出、認可

(A) If she wants him to change the light in the hallway closet. *是否要請他來填*

(B) If she reorganized the hallway closet. *她是否重整走廊櫃子*

(C) If she is planning on changing the light in the hallway closet. *是否要換*

(D) If she noticed the light is burned out in the hallway closet. *是否注意到燈燒了*

He'll not recognize me any longer. *concern ⓥ 涉及.關係到*

他不願再理睬我了. 使擔心

69. (**B**) What does the woman say?

notice
v. 注意
通知
留心

(A) That she didn't <u>notice</u> the light is out. → *The news concerns your brother.*
消息和你弟弟有關

(B) That she was going to ask the man to change it.

(C) That she is going out to buy light bulbs. *她很掛心節省能源這件事*

(D) That she is <u>concerned about</u> saving energy.

The plane was noticed to take off at six o'clock. → *Tom's poor health concerned his parents.*

70. (**A**) What will the man most likely do next?

hardware
n. 五金器具
設備

(A) Change the light bulb in the hallway closet. *他持病不好.使父母擔憂*

(B) Go down to the <u>hardware</u> store. /ˈhɑrd/

(C) Ask the woman to change the light bulb in the hallway closet. *ⓝ 關心的事*

(D) Change all the light bulbs in the house. → *That's no concern of mine.*

I know nothing about computer hardware. *unveil /e/ v.揭幕 紗 揭露*

擔心.掛念
→ *Tom expressed his concern.*
表達他的關切

PART 4

courtesy n.禮貌. 好意 殷勤

今天我們很高興要揭幕我們城市創立者 William 的真人大小雕塑

Welcome to Center Park. Today we're proud to unveil this life-size statue of our city

這個案子是由市中心文化基金會的好意捐助

founder, William Center. The funding for this project was <u>courtesy</u> of a donation from

雕刻是由當地的藝術家雕刻的—Kurt Black

the Center City Culture Foundation, and the statue was <u>sculpted</u> by a local artist, Mr.

今天很榮幸邀請到 Black 先生   *Kurt是市中心當地人*

Kurt Black. We are honored to have Mr. Black with us this morning. Kurt is a native

他來自個藝術家庭   *其中有很多人是 NYA 畢業的*

of Center City and he comes from a family of artists, many of whom graduated from the

他從 16 歲時便開始雕刻

New York Institute of Art. He has been sculpting statues since he was 16 and his work

他所有的被陳列在博物館中   *今天 Kurt 會告訴你關於他從 William*

is displayed in museums all over the world, as well. Today Kurt will tell you about

世界各地的   *的一張肖像開始雕刻. 這個過程花了好幾個月的時間*

carving this statue from an old <u>portrait</u> of William Center, a process which took several

他們在雜草叢生的地方開拓了果園

months. Please join me in welcoming Mr. Kurt Black.

They carved out an orchard where there used to be wild grass.

60

portrait /o/e 肖像.畫像   *sculp v.雕刻)*   *carve v.① 刻.雕刻) /skʌlp/ ② 開創事業.開拓 ——*

雜草叢生的地方開拓了果園

71. (C) What is true about Kurt Black?
(A) He founded Center City.
(B) His paintings are famous all over the world.
(C) He comes from a family of artists.
(D) His statue of William Center was self-financed.

72. (B) What will Kurt Black talk about?
(A) William Center.
(B) The carving of the statue.
(C) Portrait photography.
(D) New York Institute of Art.

73. (B) Who paid for the project?
(A) William Center.
(B) The Center City Cultural Foundation.
(C) Kurt Black.
(D) The New York Institute of Art.

Questions 74 through 76 are based on the following talk.

Obviously, your dishwasher is convenient. But did you also know that it's one of your best allies in keeping your kitchen safe from contaminants? The dishwasher sanitizes everything that goes in it, if you use the dry cycle. During that cycle, the internal temperature of the dishwasher reaches 170°F, which is required for sanitizing—the process of reducing harmful microbes to an acceptable level. Of course, sterilizing is something we can't aspire to in our own homes. However, you should always run anything through the dishwasher that can go into it, including glassware, flatware, plates, plastic cutting boards, and sponges. Anything that touches raw meat and fish, or their juices or blood, should be placed in the dishwasher immediately. That means if you use a sponge to wipe up the counter that's been in contact with raw meat, you should toss it right in the dishwasher and get out a clean one. At the very least, your sponges should go into the dishwasher every time you run it. Be sure to keep a backup supply on hand so you are not tempted to use a dirty one.

Handwritten notes:

found v. 建立、創辦
A good relationship has to be founded on trust.

Carve /a/ v. 雕刻 切割

*photograph /ˈfoʊtəˌɡræf/ n. 照片 v. 給~拍照
photography /fəˈtɑːɡrəfi/ n. 照相術、攝影術 使深深印入
→ The sad sight photographed itself on her mind.

*ally /əˈlaɪ/ v. 結盟 The small country allied itself to the stronger power.
/ˈælaɪ/ n. 同盟國、同盟者
Britain was an ally of America in the World War I.

*sanitize v. 給~消毒
*sterilize v. 將~殺菌

*sanitary adj. 衛生的
sanity n. 穩健
Sanity of judgement has never deserted him.
穩健的判斷沒有拋棄他 (他從未失去明確的判斷力)

74. (A) What is the main purpose of this talk? 這篇話為何? 販毒者
   (A) To inform. 告知、告發 He informed against the drug pusher.
   (B) To accuse. 控訴、指責 He accused his boss of having broken
   (C) To sell. his word.
   (D) To oppose. v.反對、反抗 He is strongly opposed to the plan.
   ə ɒz

75. (C) What does the speaker suggest? 演講者建議什麼?
sterilize (A) Washing hands frequently. 常洗手 The question is frequently asked.
ˈstɛrəˌlaɪz (B) Using cold water. 用冷水 頻繁地、屢次地
v.殺菌. (C) Using the dry cycle of the dishwasher. 用洗碗機的乾循環
使消毒 (D) Sterilizing all food used in the kitchen. 幫廚房所有的東西殺菌

76. (B) What is required for sanitizing? 消毒需要什麼?
   (A) Raw meat or fish. 生肉或魚
＊retain (B) 170°F.   ＊ a great deal of
ɪˈten (C) Glassware. 玻璃製品   good amount of }+UC
v.保留、保持 (D) Sponges. 海棉   number of +C

記住 Concentrated study will help you to retain knowledge.

Questions 77 through 99 refer to the following excerpt from a seminar.

我們該如何吸引且留住客戶呢   . Massive Mart 這樣的零售超商而言
How do we attract and retain customers? For a retail superstore like Massive Mart,
這可能是首需要強調的問題   就, 我們很注重細節
it's probably the most important question to address. First, we pay a great deal of
像商店的外觀(即視覺)   燈光
attention to detail—the store's immediate physical appearance, the lighting, and
特別是清潔度   清潔對我來說是件大事   因為這是我去某地時首先
especially the cleanliness. Cleanliness is a big thing for me, since it's the first thing I
要看的事情   停車場是否乾淨   標示是否清楚、好閱讀
look for when I go somewhere. Is the parking lot clean? Are the signs visible and easy
再來我投資我們的員工   福利政策很好   我們
to read? Second, we invest in our employees. The benefits package is great. We pay
我們付薪水很大方   每個月發獎金   我們提供有結構的退休計畫
generous salaries, we pay monthly bonuses, and we offer a structured retirement
我們相信滿足的工作人員 = 滿足的客戶   我們只採用(下)
plan. We believe that satisfied workers equal satisfied customers. We just introduced
可以全員出動的事 =All hands to the pumps.   →上班尖峰時間, 4~8點
something we call All Hands On Deck. In the busiest hours, from 4 p.m. to 8 p.m., we
我們停止所有客戶看不見的活動   像是後面房間卸貨   和組織(排陳列)
stop all activity that the customers can't see, like back room unloading and organizing,
並把每位銷售人員和收銀人員到外面工作   這真的是實際的
and put every salesclerk and cashier out on the floor. It's really that hands-on
讓大家會想回來的體驗   我們每週大約收到50,000各
experience that makes people want to come back. We hear from about 50,000 客戶的回音
customers each week, and they rate us on a number of attributes. So far, they tell us
他們評了我們說對好質. 目前為止, 他們說
that we're doing the right thing.   我們正在做對的事。

＊attribute   ＊introduce
æ ə   v.介紹、引見
n.特質   引進 Coffee was introduced into England from the Continent.
attribute   提出、推行 The vice chairman of the committee introduced
               a topic for discussion.
v.歸因於
He attributed his good health to exercise.   副議長提出議題讓大家討論

62

77. (A) Who is most likely the speaker?
corporate (A) A corporate manager. 公司經理
ɔ ɔ I (B) A sales clerk. 銷售人員
adj.法人的 (C) A cashier. 櫃枱人員
團體的 (D) A parking lot attendant. 停車場服務人員
公司的 teffort 共同的努力 + property 公司財產

* a attendant
to 傾人
n.侍從、侍者
adj.侍候的、護理的
an attendant nurse 隨侍護士

78. (D) What is the speaker talking about?
retail (A) A shipping company. 貨運公司
n.零售 (B) A parking garage. 停車庫
adj.零售的 (C) A marketing agency. 行銷公司
retailer n.零售店、零售商 (D) A retail store. 零售店

→ One of the difficulties attendant on shift work is lack of sleep.
海班工作制帶來的困難之一是睡眠不足

79. (D) Which of the following is NOT an employee benefit?
generous (A) Generous salaries. 大方的薪水
adj.大方的 (B) Monthly bonuses. 每月紅利
慷慨的 (C) A retirement plan. 退休計劃
大量的 (D) Free parking. 免費停車
She gave me a generous lunch. 她請我吃一頓豐盛の午餐.

* Please clear up the problem for me.
請為我解釋問題
We hope to clear the matter up quickly.
澄清, 水落石出

Questions 80 through 82 refer to the following news report.

This is Coralynn Guest with a KBUT news update. We have some spectacular video
footage of firefighters working to contain the forest fire at Mount Holyoke. As you can
see, the inferno continues to rage out of control. A spokesman for the Mount Holyoke
Forest Reserve estimates that 30% of the fire is under containment. Investigators
have not yet determined the cause of the fire, which has already caused an estimated
$500 million in damage to homes in the Mount Holyoke area. There is good news for
the fire crews as Mother Nature will provide some relief. A look at the KBUT weather
map shows a storm front headed our way this afternoon and evening, expected to
bring heavy rain and thundershowers. The skies should begin to clear up tomorrow
evening, and the wind will die down, giving those firefighters a break. Meanwhile, the
weekend is expected to be clear and dry. In other news, the financial markets are
volatile at this hour after hitting a morning low, followed by a tremendous buying surge
that set record highs on both the NASDAQ and Dow Jones. Finally in sports, the
Dodgers lost to the Reds 3-2 in extra innings last night and have tonight off before
hosting Seattle tomorrow. I'm Coralynn Guest for KBUT news.

我們有一些引人注目的影片.
消防隊員在控制Holyoke山的森林大火
這場火持續擴大失去控制
Holyoke山保育區的發言人說
大火 預估30%的大火在控制之中
調查人員
尚未決定(確認)火火發生的原因
這火災已經造成估計5億美元
在當地住宅的損害 對於打火英雄而言
有大好消息這些緩解是個好消息
來看一下KBUT氣象圖
顯示有暴風雨今天下午和晚上朝我們的方向來. 預期暴風來
大雨和雷陣雨 明天開始天空會放晴
傍晚 給打火弟兄一個喘息
同時, 周末預計晴朗且乾燥 其他新聞方面 財經市場
目前動盪今早達到低點 在一個不穩 NASDAQ和Dow Jones
都是新高的購買潮
最後體育新聞方面
Dodgers 輸給 Reds 3比2 在昨晚的延長賽中. 明天對戰西雅圖後今晚休息

host
對戰
* volatile
adj.善變的、易變的 = fickle

n.大浪、激增
奔騰、蜂擁而至、洶湧

Every time a bus came,
the crowd surged forward.

GO ON TO THE NEXT PAGE.

80. (C) Where was this report most likely being broadcast? 這篇報導是在哪裡播放的？
   (A) Radio. 電台
   (B) Internet. 網路
   (C) Television. 電視
   (D) Public Address system. 公眾演講系統 / 稱呼 He addressed her as Miss Mannie.

*address
演說 He is going to address the meeting. 向大會做演說
對~說話 He is addressing the chairman.

81. (B) What happened at Mount Holyoke?
雷陣雨 (A) A baseball game. 棒球比賽
thunder (B) A forest fire. 森林大火
   shower (C) A thunderstorm. 大雷雨.
毛毛雨: drizzle, light rain (D) A traffic jam. 塞車

*jam
n. 果醬. 擁擠. 堵塞 v. 塞進. 壓碎. 卡住
The key jammed in the lock.
* traffic (n) 交通, 運輸. 交流
I don't want any traffic with him.

82. (D) What will most likely happen tonight?
contain (A) The Dodgers will go to Seattle. 道奇會去西雅圖
a le (B) The fire will be contained. 火被控制
hold (C) The skies will clear up. 天空放晴
v. 包含. 容納. 控制 (D) The storm front will bring rain. 鋒面會帶來雨水
* curb 人行道旁的路邊   放晴. 清理. 澄清

(v1) 交易, 非法買賣
→ The man trafficked with the natives for ivory.
* human trafficking
人口販賣

Questions 83 through 85 refer to the following announcement.
Please clear up the problem for me.   很榮幸的宣布

This is Oliver Hamilton, director of Tulsa Community Services and I'm pleased to
宣布我們年度慈善商品收集的活動   下週二15號. 卡車會部屬在整個城市
announce our annual collection of charity items. Trucks will be deployed across the
我們找尋捐贈的乾淨舊衣服(二手)
city next Tuesday, the 15th. We're looking for donations of clean used clothing,
廚具   家庭用品   書本和遊戲. 保存良好的   我們不接受
cookware, household utensils, and books and games in good condition. We cannot
電腦或是大型電器   我們請你把要捐的物品放置在前門廊或是
accept computers or large appliances. We ask that you place donated items on your
你家門前路邊(E)   15號早上7:00以前放好
front porch or the curb in front of your house. Set them out by seven in the morning on
並且標註CS 大寫在物品上   我們會在5點以前取走
the 15th, and mark them "CS" in large letters. We will pick them up sometime before
如果你有任何疑問或是想安排不同的取貨日期
five p.m. If you have any questions or want to schedule a pickup for a different date,
please call 800-456-1122 between eight a.m. and five p.m. Monday through Friday.
Thank you, and have a great day.   請在週間1~5, 早上8:00~下午5:00之間來電
promote. v. 促進. 提升. 引起. 宣傳   謝謝, 祝你有愉快的一天

83. (B) What is the main purpose of this announcement?
remind (A) To promote a business. 宣傳一門生意   * solicit
提醒 (B) To solicit charity donations. 請求慈善捐款   v. 請求, 乞求
使想起 (C) To explain a policy. 解釋政策   They are busy soliciting votes.
   (D) To remind someone of an appointment.   他們正忙著拉選票
      提醒某人有預約
└ The story reminds me of an experience I once   * appliance   n. 器具. 用具. 裝置
   had.   to | ply 折
這個故事讓我想起一次親身經歷

64

84. (C) When are the trucks scheduled to be <u>deployed</u>?

deploy
v. 展開
部署

(A) Monday through Friday.
(B) Anytime before five p.m.
(C) On Tuesday the 15th.
(D) <u>Throughout</u> the month.

*throughout
遍布、貫穿、從頭到尾

The feeling persisted throughout the day.
這種感覺持續了一整天

85. (B) What is not accepted?

apply v.
appliance n.
器具、設備
·應用

(A) <u>Household</u> <u>utensils</u>.
(B) Large appliances.
(C) <u>Used</u> clothing.
(D) Cookware.

*Chapter 11
美國破產法的其中一條

*household adj. 家庭的、普通的
為人所知的

→ He is a household legendary figure. 他是個家喻戶曉的傳奇性人物

Questions 86 through 88 *refer to the following talk.*

In my opinion, investments are based on your tolerance for risk. In other words, not just how much money can you stand to lose, but how much are you willing to lose? The stock market is clearly the fast track to success. The upside of investing in stocks is that you can profit in a short time, but it's also a risk. You could get killed in the stock market faster than you can say, "<u>Chapter 11</u>." I've made and lost so many fortunes in the stock market that I've lost track. Therefore, I personally wouldn't invest in stocks with money I figure I'm going to need in the next five years. Bonds have less risk than stocks, but the downside is that the return is small and slow in coming. You know, folks, it may sound like some kind of folksy, down-home wisdom, but I measure the safety of my investments by how much sleep I lose worrying about them. Let me give you an example of an investment that <u>kept me awake</u> all night.

*awake 喚醒、激起、意識到 → We must awake to our responsibilities.

86. (A) Who is the speaker most likely to be?

therapy
n. 治療
療法

(A) A successful investment broker.
(B) A sleep <u>therapist</u>.
(C) An author of <u>folk</u> tales.
(D) A <u>serial</u> killer.

*serial adj. 連續的、一系列的
/SIRIəl/ + numbers + book

*cereal n. 穀物
/SIRIəl/

87. (B) What does the speaker say about the stock market?

risky
危險的
冒險的
大膽的

(A) It is <u>lethal</u>. 致命的
(B) It is <u>risky</u>.
(C) It is <u>sleepy</u>.
(D) It is <u>folksy</u>.

I feel sleepy.
am
to make sb. sleepy 使某人犯睏
sleepyhead 懶鬼、瞌睡蟲

GO ON TO THE NEXT PAGE.

88. (D) How does the speaker measure the risk of his investments? 演講者如何評估
他的投資風險？
measure up 符合標準
(A) By hand. 用手 (v.測量,估量,打量)
(B) By how much money he makes or loses. 他賺了或者損失 3 多少錢
(C) By keeping track of his fortunes. 一直追蹤(掌握)他有了多少財產
(D) By how much sleep he loses worrying about them. 他因為擔心而少睡了多少

She measured the stranger with her eyes. 双眼打量陌生人

Questions 89 through 91 refer to the following introduction.

今晚的高潮要開始了 重點,高潮處(下) 我是RB, 我是今晚活動的主持人
OK, now it's time for the highlight of the evening. My name's Ralph Baker, and I'm the emcee for tonight's program. It's my privilege to introduce our featured speaker, Mr. Phil Spitz. Ten years ago, Phil started brewing beer that was based on his grandfather Ben's recipe. If you haven't heard of Ben's Beer yet, you soon will. Last year Mr. Spitz signed a distribution agreement with a national distributor, and soon Ben's Beer will be a household name. Tonight Phil, who's only 26, will discuss what it's like to be a successful entrepreneur at such a young age, and where he will take his young company from here. Mr. Spitz will speak for about 60 minutes. Please save all your questions for the end of his speech, when there will be a 30-minute question-and-answer session. If you have a question for Phil at that time, raise your hand, and one of our ushers will bring you a wireless microphone so that everyone in the room will be able to hear you. So without further ado, please welcome Mr. Phil Spitz.

主持人, 司儀
說我的榮幸介紹主講人PS先生
private law → 特權,榮幸 Phil開始他的釀酒業,用他
爺爺Ben傳下來的食譜 如果你還沒有聽過Ben Beer,你很快就會聽到
去年 他簽了個派送合同和全國的乙送商,馬上 Ben Beer 就會是個家喻戶曉的名字
今晚,只有26歲的Phil,會討論如何成為成功的企業家
在如此年輕的時候,而且他將會帶領公司走向哪裡
他大約會演講約60分鐘 請把問題留到最後
演講結束時 到時將會有30分鐘的Q&A環節
如果你到時有問題要問他 請舉手 我們其中一位
接待員(服務人員)會拿無線的麥克風給你,所以房裡的每個人能夠聽到你
廢話不多說

(*) privilege
n.特權 v.給予特權
榮耀 免除
→ This pass will privilege you to attend the closed hearing.
有這張通行證
你可以出席
這個不公開的公聽會.

89. (D) Who is being introduced? 誰被介紹
scummy ↑ 卑鄙的+
(A) An elderly beer maker. 一位年長的啤酒製造者
(B) A famous politician. 有名的政客
(C) A corporate executive. 公司的執行長
(D) A young entrepreneur. 年輕的企業家 /ˌɑntrəprəˈnɜr/↑
politician 可鄙的政客

(*) highlight

90. (B) What will the speaker talk about? 演講者會討論什麼 n.
conviction ə I
n.信仰
+politician 有信仰的政治家
(A) His education. 他的教育 ≠religion 狂熱的愛好 v. =emphasize
(B) His business. 他的生意 He makes a religion of = stress
(C) His religion. 他的宗教 watching basketball. = underline
(D) His family. 他的家庭 觀眾何時可以問問題 highlighter n.螢光筆

91. (A) When can the audience ask questions?
audience n.聽眾 觀眾 讀者群
(A) At the end of the speech. 演讀結束後
(B) Before the speech begins. 演講開始前
(C) 30 minutes later. 30分鐘後
(D) There will be no questions allowed. 不準問問題

→ religious 虔誠的
Our parents were very religious and patriotic.
e I æ I 愛國的

The book have a large audience.

66

大家注意一下這裡好嗎?　　Denver出發、預計10:57到達的718巴士

May I have your attention, please? Bus 7-1-8 from Denver, scheduled to arrive at

遇到了技術的問題, 目前在城郊拋錨了　　　　(上)

10:57, is experiencing mechanical difficulties and is currently stalled just outside the

一台新巴士在路上　　零載乘客們, 並且預計大約一小時會到達這裡

city limits. A new bus is en route to transport passengers and is expected to be here

　　　　　　　　"on the way　造成延遲非常抱歉　　同時在等718去

in about an hour. We apologize for the delay. Meanwhile, passengers waiting for bus

LV、LA的乘客很歡迎請於休息室免費用餐

7-1-8 to Las Vegas and Los Angeles are invited to have a free meal in our lounge.

在用餐櫃台處拿到午餐　　　　　提供午餐和飲料　　我們門的(下)

Show your boarding pass at the dining counter to receive lunch and a beverage, on us.

如果你打算要在LV, LA搭轉接巴士

If you are a 7-1-8 passenger planning to catch connecting buses in Las Vegas or Los

我們會試圖安排多的巴士, 並避免更多的延遲

Angeles, we are phoning those stations and trying to arrange for extra buses to meet

困這成你的不便, 我們再次致歉　　　　請注意

you and avoid further delays. We apologize again for this inconvenience. Please note

我們的準點率超過90%　　　　如果你想要退款因為這次的延遲

that our on-time rate is better than 90 percent. If you would like a refund due to this

postpone延遲 =delay =defer = suspend = stall = put off = hold over

postponement, please take your boarding pass to the customer service desk in the

請拿著你的登車證(車票)到車站後面的客服櫃台

back of the station.

boarding house 供食宿的宿舍, boarding school 寄宿學校　boarding kennel 寄宿寵物店(高級)

92. (D) Where does this announcement take place? 這篇宣佈是在哪裡舉行的? take place

    (A) On the radio. 電台裡

    (B) At a business meeting. 商務會議　(n.) 原因, 理由, 目標　(發生出現)

    (C) On television. 電視　　You have no cause to complain.

    (D) In a bus station.　　World peace is a cause we should

Cause (v)導致, 引起 I'm afraid I'm causing you much trouble.　　all work for.

93. (C) What caused the 7-1-8 bus to be late? 是什麼引起了718公車延遲　世界和平是我們

parade (A) A snow storm in Denver. Denver有暴風雪　　　都該努力的目標

遊行 (B) Heavy traffic in Los Angeles. LA有塞車

招搖 (C) Mechanical trouble on the outskirts of the city. 城市的郊區有技術性問題

炫耀 (D) Parades in Las Vegas. LA有遊行　　= in the suburbs of

The myths paraded as modern science 迷思假冒成現代科學.

94. (B) What should listeners do if they want a refund? 如果他們想退款該怎麼做?

complain (A) Take the 7-1-8 bus to Las Vegas. 搭718巴士

(v)抱怨, 投訴 (B) Bring their boarding passes to customer service. 帶登車證到客服部

complaint (C) Have lunch in the lounge. 在休息室吃午餐

(n.) (D) Complain to the manager. 向經理抱怨　　★我請客 It's on me.

stall　　　　　　　　　　　　　　　　　　　　　　It's my treat.

v. 使熄火, 使拋錨, 使失速　　　　　　　　　餐廳招待 It's on the house.

All inexperienced pilot can easily stall his plane.

　使動彈不得　　　　, 把~關入畜舍

We were stalled in the mud.　The cows were stalled in the barn for the night.

Questions 95 through 97 refer to the following advertisement and price list.

It's June and that means Buffalo Jed's Furniture is hosting its annual summer sale, and right now our very popular dining room table is on sale for 75% off the original price! This deal is valid for in-store purchases only. You can just pick it up from the store. All of the parts are included in one small box. Our customers love this dining room table because it can be assembled at home quickly and easily. Just log on to our website to access our simple assembly instructions. Don't miss out on this deal! Come visit us at Buffalo Jed's Furniture today, where the prices just couldn't get any lower.

95. (B) Look at the graphic. What is the sale price of the table being described?
- (A) $18.00.
- (B) $25.00.
- (C) $27.50.
- (D) $30.00.

Item	Original Price	Sale Price
Dining room table	$100.00	$25.00
Coffee table	$54.00	$18.00
Patio table	$90.00	$30.00
Kitchen table	$110.00	$27.50

96. (C) According to the speaker, why do customers like the table?
- (A) It is hand-made.
- (B) It is available in many colors.
- (C) It is easy to assemble.
- (D) It is inexpensive.

97. (A) What does the speaker say can be found on a website?
- (A) Some instructions.
- (B) Some recipes.
- (C) A warranty.
- (D) A coupon.

68

awareness

我打電話來是要詢問，我們討論幫忙募款的乳癌提醒活動。(注意、了解、意識)

Hey Lindsey, this is Dylan. I'm calling about the music festival we've been planning to
(子)
help raise funds for breast cancer awareness. Got a problem here, Lindsey. Have you
你有看天氣預報嗎？　飛明顯地　　　　活動那天天氣反常的熱
seen the weather forecast? Apparently, it's supposed to be unseasonably hot on the
　　　　　　　　　　　　　　　　超過102度　即使以此使用
day we were planning to hold our event. Over 102 degrees. Even with the use of
工業級電扇　　　　　　沒有表演者會願意在那樣的情況下表演
industrial fans on stage, none of the performers will want to play under those
　　　　　　　我希望你把團隊聚集起來，把事情處理好，選一個替換日期
conditions. So, I'd like you to get the team together tomorrow sometime to get things
adj.交替的、輪流的、相隔的　　　　　　　　　　　　紅字＝輕小的、不重要的
in order for an alternate date. Could you organize that? Mostly minor planning
adjustments that we'll need to make.　你可以安排嗎？　大多是小小的安排調整
→ They saw each other on alternate Sundays. 每隔一星期日見一次　　　*fund
98. (D)　What event is being discussed? 正在討論什麼活動？　　(n.)資金、募款、積累
grand
adj.宏偉的　(A) A grand opening. 盛大開幕；grand holiday
　　　　　(B) A charity walk. 慈善健走　快樂的假期　a pension fund
盛大的、偉大的(C) A trip to the zoo.　　　　　　　　　trust
a grand house / a grand prize 大獎　(D) A music festival. 音樂會　(v.)資助：The school is being privately funded.
99. (C)　Look at the graphic. Which day was the event originally scheduled for? 活動最一開始是預計在哪天舉辦？
graphic　(A) Thursday.　　部分有雲　　　adv.起初、原來、獨創地、新穎地
adj.　　　(B) Friday.　　　並有零星雷雨
生動的　　(C) Saturday.　　　　　　　　　　　The crowd scattered
寫實的　　(D) Sunday.　　scatter　v.撒播、分散 when the police charged.
圖解的　　　　　　　thunderstorm n.雷雨　警察衝過來時、人群潰散
graphic design　　　　　　　　　　　　　　　　開了

CHARLOTTESVILLE WEEKEND WEATHER FORECAST			
Thursday	Friday	Saturday	Sunday
Cloudy and humid	Partly cloudy with scattered thunderstorms	Extreme heat advisory	Sunny with onshore winds
Hi: 95 / Lo: 78	Hi: 97 / Lo: 83	Hi: 103 / Lo: 88	Hi: 96 / Lo: 80

平面設計
多雲且潮溼　　　超級熱浪警告　晴天+吹向陸地的海風
humid = moist　　advise v.勸告、告知 提出建議
= damp　　　　　Please advise us of any change in your plan.
= wet　　　　　　We advised him against acting in haste.
= muggy　　　　　勸他不要匆忙行事

*industrious
adj.勤勉的　勤勞的

If you are industrious you can finish the job before dark.

100. (A)　What does the speaker ask the listener to do?　　　*華氏 Fahrenheit
= hard-working(A) Arrange a meeting. 安排會議　　　　　　攝氏 Celsius
= dilligent　(B) Contact scheduled performers. 聯絡安排的表演者
= tireless　(C) Rent industrial fans. 租工業用風扇　industrial
= energetic　(D) Print new tickets. 印新的票　adj.工業的、產業的　+machine 工業用的機器

READING TEST

In the Reading test, you will read a variety of texts and answer several different types of reading comprehension questions. The entire Reading test will last 75 minutes. There are three parts, and directions are given for each part. You are encouraged to answer as many questions as possible within the time allowed.

You must mark your answers on the separate answer sheet. Do not write your answers in your test book.

PART 5

Directions: A word or phrase is missing in each of the sentences below. Four answer choices are given below each sentence. Select the best answer to complete the sentence. Then mark the letter (A), (B), (C), or (D) on your answer sheet.

101. Do you know when the boss is ------- New York?
(A) going at
(B) come to
(C) leaving for
(D) arrived in

102. The winning lottery numbers will be announced at -------.
(A) seven o'clock
(B) seventeen
(C) the seventh
(D) the seven

103. Researchers have ------- determined whether playing video games changes the brain's chemistry.
(A) yet
(B) not yet
(C) while
(D) not while

104. The clerk's job is to handle cash -------.
(A) transformations
(B) transportations
(C) transactions
(D) transplantations

105. I'm sorry, sir, but I can't give you a refund without a -------.
(A) statement
(B) reference
(C) bill
(D) receipt

106. The news of Ronald's recovery brought a smile ------- my face.
(A) in
(B) on
(C) by
(D) to

107. No one knows how long it will take to ------- the wildfires in Arizona.
(A) malnourish
(B) distinguish
(C) extinguish
(D) establish

108. The bus will ------- in front of the library entrance.
(A) throw us up
(B) stick us around
(C) drop us off
(D) pick us apart

GO ON TO THE NEXT PAGE.

13

109. Don't take what Jim says at -------. He's been known to stretch the truth.

(A) face value *不要聽他字面上的意思。他一直*
(B) a discount *face-off 攤牌 對立 都愛扭曲事實*
(C) shelf life *He and the manager had a face-off,*
(D) great risk *but nothing came of it. 和經理對抗但*

懊惱 個性 保存期限

→ 我們需要和供應商聯絡。有空時打個電話 沒有

110. We need to contact our supplier. ------- the call when you have a minute.

(A) Take ✗ face value *表面的意思*
(B) Make *surface n. 面 表面* *efface*
(C) Give *deface v. (外表)損壞* *v. 削除. 抹*
(D) Place *除*

我們試試路底那家飯店, 這家全客滿了。

111. Let's try that hotel down the street. This one is fully ~~booked~~

(A) set *acquisition n. 獲得. 獲得物*
(B) acquired *acquire = gain = earn*
(C) booked *= get = secure*
(D) close *= obtain*

說家張遠 覺得孤寂

112. James is far ~~from~~ home and feeling lonely. *119(B) revolve around*

(A) at *旋轉, 以...為中心*
(B) of *A baby's life revolves around it's mother.*
(C) with *She has no outside interest at all,*
(D) from *her life revolves around her husband.*

這休的第一次. 緊張沒有什麼好丟臉的

113. It's your first time. There's nothing shameful about ------- nervous. *borne*

(A) to be *介 tV-ing* *bran → bore → born*
(B) has been *bear in mind 牢記在心*
(C) being *Bear in mind that you'll have to*
(D) you're *practice economy. 要厲行節約*

他決定不讓任何事情阻擋他的成功

114. He was determined to let nothing *get in the way* of his success.

(A) go by the book *照規矩做事*
(B) fall by the wayside *半途而廢*
(C) get in the way *阻擋*
(D) look for an outlet *找到出b (出路)*

Hey, you're in my way,
get out of my way.

115. ------- both sides agree to settle the dispute, there's no guarantee the truce will last. *即使雙方同意平息紛爭*

(A) Only if *也沒有保障這場休戰會持續*
(B) Provided that
(C) Even adv. 甚至 *→ 只要*
(D) Even if *即使. 假使*

什麼結果.

116. Excuse me, miss. There ------- be a fly in my soup. *不好意思, 好像有隻蒼蠅在我的湯裡* *appears to*

(A) seemed
(B) seemingly = apparently *明顯地*
(C) apparently = outwardly
(D) appears to *表面上地. 看起來地* *= seems to*

117. You need to register in order to open an e-mail *account* *要開新帳號要先註冊*

(A) setting ✗ account n. 帳號. 戶頭. 客戶
(B) file *→ accountable adj. 有解釋義務的*
(C) account *account for (應負責的)*
(D) direction *解釋. 說明 = There is no account for*

118. The man *adv.* spilled his coffee. *taste.*

(A) by accident *人口味不同*
(B) accidentally *人各有所好.*
(C) designed to *討意*
(D) with intention *介 + N 的片語只能放 D, 之後* *= intentionally*

119. Tim's illness seems to have -------. He's feeling much better now. *Tim的不舒服好像*

(A) borne in mind *快走完全程了 (快結束了)。*
(B) run its course *他現在覺得好多了*
(C) revolved around *→ 走完全程 = 自然結束*
(D) lightened his load *減輕負擔*

120. The maestro's performance received mixed ~~reviews~~ */maɪstro/* *大師的表演收到各種的評價*

(A) tests *term*
(B) studies *course paper*
(C) essays *篇, 小論文* *research*
(D) reviews *dissertation 碩博* *✗ review*
thesis 博碩 *v. 檢查. 評論*
回顧. 檢閱
n. 意思和 v. 一樣 *英 美*
多一個 "評論文章"

14

121. Many supermarkets are now providing customers with ------- checkout lanes, eliminating the need for cashiers.

eliminate v. 除去.淘汰

D

自學← (A) self-esteem 很多超市現在都提供
(B) self-styled 客人自助結帳的走道
自學 (C) self-taught 排除對櫃枱人員的需求
自助 (D) self-service
服務

122. Would you mind ------- late tonight?

C
(A) stayed 你介意留晚一點嗎?
(B) stay
(C) staying
(D) stays

玩任何遊戲.你需要先知道規則~

123. In order to play any game, first you must understand the rules.

C
(A) runes 神秘的記號
(B) rulers 尺
(C) rules =regulation role n.角色.作用
(D) rumors /01

Rumors has it that~ 謠傳說~

124. I'm really excited about our ski trip this weekend. I can't wait to hit the slopes! n.斜坡 我很期待這週末的滑雪

D
(A) hug 我忍不住要滑斜坡了!
(B) hold
(C) house n.房子 v.留宿.囤積
(D) hit 達到.碰到

hang tough
hang in there
go all the way
go for the gold

125. The saying goes that you can't make a(n) omelet without breaking eggs.

C
(A) baby 俗話說你不能不打破蛋
(B) record 就做出歐姆蛋
(C) omelet （沒有失不可能有得）
(D) deal

炒蛋: scrambled eggs
滷蛋: braised egg
玉子燒: tamagoyaki
鐵蛋: iron egg
鹹蛋: salted duck egg

omelet 裡面可以加
mushroom 蘑菇
ham , cheese , onion
bacon , tomato , corn
green 青椒

126. Skeptics say computer models used to predict global warming are prone to error.

C
(A) pound 多疑論者說.以前用來預測
(B) pressed 全球暖化的電腦模型可能
(C) prone 是錯的. be prone to < N./V-ing
(D) pure 有~的傾向

127. The workers threatened to go on strike if their demands were not met.

C
試用.審問← (A) trial 工人們威脅要罷工如果沒有達到
(B) maternity 要求.
(C) strike → call
(D) duty 責任 stage] a strike 發動.組

n.產科醫院
母性
a maternity dress

put down / suppress 鎮壓

128. After a thorough inspection, I found several potential safety hazards in my 危險 work area, which I reported to my -------.

B
(A) therapist 徹底檢查後.我發現幾個潛在
(B) supervisor 的安全疑慮在我的工作區
(C) dietitian 我向我的主管報告
(D) auditor

試驗主.查帳員 → 營養學者

129. Your exercise program may seem difficult now, but stick with it and I promise you'll see positive results. 你的運動課程可能看起來

A
(A) stick with it 有些困難.但堅持下去
(B) drop it on 你會看到正面的結果
(C) seal it with
(D) it means it → 用~封住

130. I haven't spoken to my sister since September. 我從9月開始就沒和我妹

D
(A) from 說話了
(B) until
(C) by since+特定時間點
(D) since for + 時間長度
from A 時 to B 時

→ I've worked here since 1999.
→ I've worked here for 20 years.
→ I work from dawn to dusk.

GO ON TO THE NEXT PAGE.

PART 6

Directions: Read the texts that follow. A word, phrase, or sentence is missing in parts of each text. Four answer choices are given below each of the texts. Select the best answer to complete the text. Then mark the letter (A), (B), (C), or (D) on your answer sheet.

*fund n. 基金.資金.專款 v.提供資金.積累

Questions 131-134 refer to the news article.

Who is funding the project?

board of foreign trade 國貿局
board of governors 理事會.董事會
board of education 教育董事會
board of directors 董事會
board of supervisors 監察委員會

電腦基金同意.(同意發放電腦基金)

Computer Funds Approved by Board of Supervisors

technician n. 技術員 technical adj.工藝的.科技的 工藝
技師 技術的 n. 技術.科技.術語

THOUSAND OAKS (May 23) — New technology is coming -------
新科技要來囉   131.

the students of Thousand Oaks Unified School District. On Friday,

Mayor Cheyenne Loomis announced that her "Future Now" proposal
declare, state, proclaim, broadcast

has been approved by the Board of Supervisors.

↑承接和預算有關的句子   這個案子撥出每間學校20萬
-------. The program allots $200,000 to each school in the city for the
132.   ∂ a

purchase of computers. Students will be allowed to take home
學生被允許偶爾帶筆電和平板回家.做特殊作業和

laptops and tablets ------- for special assignments and class projects,
133.

be available

but they will normally ------- to the students only during school hours.
134.

但通常只有在學校有開的時候 才能借

*allow
∂ av

v.允許.提供 → The windfall allowed me to buy a house. 意外之財讓我可以買
認可.承諾 → The judge allowed the claim.法官同意了請求.   房子.

He allowed that they were right.

131. (A) to
A (B) at   *discount →現金付款打9折
   (C) from   n. 折扣: We give a 10% discount for cash.
   (D) on
        不全信: The author's conclusions must be
        taken at a discount.
        作者的結論

132. (A) The desks will be purchased at a discount
D   rate 這張桌子可以用折扣價格買到
   (B) The final decision is expected next month 最後的決定
   (C) Nevertheless, the mayor remains content 預定下個月公布
        with the decision
   (D) The vote took place on Wednesday, May 21

投票發生在5/21.周三

nevertheless adv.仍然.不過.然而

市長維持滿意這個決定(的想法.的態度)

133. (A) occasionally 偶爾地
A (B) exceptionally 特殊地.例外地
   (C) finally
   (D) supposedly 可能.大概.推測

134. (A) are available
C (B) not available   作者的結論
   (C) be available   不全信.
   (D) were availed

We can't act on your
我們不能照你的 advice.

意見去辦.但謝你
Nevertheless, thank you
for giving it.

*frustrate v. 挫敗   frustrating   * utilize
in vain   v. 受挫的   adj. 令人沮喪的   = use
徒勞   www.theadagency.com/home   = employ

① 雇人
② 利用: How do you employ your spare time?
③ 使忙於
→ The children employed themselves in painting.

THE **AD** AGENCY

我們來面對損宾吧。到導你的生意有時讓人很沮喪。貿易展和行業論壇仍是個有效的
Let's face it: Promoting your business can be frustrating. Trade shows   (好的)
= place
and industry forums are still ------ useful venues for meeting potential clients.
135.   地方來認認潛在客戶。   * critical
adj. 嚴重的, 危急的
However   但是, 網路變成了最重要的
------, the Internet has become the most critical advertising and   批評的, 關鍵性的
136.   廣告和行銷出口   = crucial = decisive
= urgent
marketing outlet.

廣告公司利用網路和傳統廣告方法來宣傳客戶所提供的東西 (商品 or 服務)
The Ad Agency utilizes both traditional commercial outlets and the Internet
請看后者有關的   降了事有的, 怨擇的
to promote clients' offerings. ------. In addition to exceptional
傳統廣告   廣告公司有專家可以幫助你線上曝光最大化
137.
traditional advertising, The Ad Agency has the expertise to help you to
optimize
------ your online presence. Why wait? Choose our award-winning firm
138.   出現, 在場, 存在, 眼前   何需等待, 選擇我們這間得過獎的公司來強化你們公司的
to strengthen your company's image today!   形象吧?

A nowhere
adv. She goes almost nowhere.
n. She had nowhere to go.   137(A) 行銷專家給出衝突的建議
(B) 傳統的方法有最好的影響
Starting from nowhere, he became a star in a few years.   (C) 我們可以為你的生意想出不相同的計畫

135. (A) evenly   ⚹ Otherwise
B (B) still   adv. 在其他情況下
(C) soon
(D) nowhere up (conj. 否則)

adj. 不同的
136. (A) However
A (B) To demonstrate   It's quite
(C) Otherwise   safe, otherwise
(D) As a result   I wouldn't do it.
這相當安全
不然我不會做的 ⚹ opt → wish
optimism 樂觀
optimist 樂觀議者

137. (A) Marketing professionals give conflicting advice
C (B) Traditional methods have the best impact
(C) We can develop a diverse plan for your business 我們最近改變了我們的服務條款。
wish
(D) We have recently changed our terms of service

138. (A) optimal adj. 最理想的
D (B) optimum adj. 最適宜的, n. 最佳條件
(C) optimization n. 最佳化, 最優化
(D) optimize 表示要觀, 發揮最大功能
/ˈɑptəmaɪˈzeʃən/
↓
I need someone who can optimize my computer
as it seems to have many glitches.
希望有人可以優化我的電腦, 因為好像有很多問題
漏洞

GO ON TO THE NEXT PAGE.

✱ manufacture ⓥ製造,捏造,虛構,加工 → who manufactured the rumor?
mænjə fæktʃx
ⓝ製造,產品 = products 給員工的重要消息　誰編造這種謠言的
merchandise IMPORTANT NEWS The company manufactures cars.
製造業 FOR TOXXICO MANUFACTURING STAFF ✱ sort v.分類,排選

我們很榮幸宣佈新的分類包裝設備(設在SS廠的)目前已完成. Can't you sort the good from bad?

We are pleased to announce that the installation of new sorting and
高興的,滿意的
packing equipment in our Sarasota Springs plant is now complete.

新的機器會改善工作順暢度,藉由生產時的完成度
The new machines ------- work flow by allowing for complete
will improve
彈性,不用停下來並 重新安裝工具
n.適應性,彈性 39. flexible adj.可彎曲的,可變通的
flexibility in production without having to stop and retool.

有5台分類+3台包裝各種尺寸 We need a foreign policy that is more flexible. 我們需要
With five sorting and three packing machines of ------- sizes, we
更有彈性的
我們預期可以滿足更廣的訂單,在短時間內,從小量到大量 140.
expect to be able to fill a wider range of orders, from small to very 外交政策
upgrade
large on short notice. This ------- is an important way to ensure that
n.製造業,工業 adj.製造的 141. 這次的升級是確保公司持續保持塑膠業
Toxxico Manufacturing continues to be a leader in the plastic 領導地位的重要方法
fabrication industry.

↑和新機器有關的(A) GM.主管這次努力的人(設備升級)將會聯絡你們給你們
------- Geoff Monteith, who is managing this effort, will contact each 細節.
142. ✱ anticipate v.預期,期序,佔先
before　e take
of you soon with details. anticipation n.
→n.製造,捏造,謊言
fabricate participate v.→ participation n. 參與
æ ɪ e emancipate v→ emancipation n. 解放,解涘
v.製造,建造,組裝,偽造

139. (A) have been improved
C   (B) were improving
     (C) will improve
     (D) improvement

141. (A) contract 合約 → The new machine
B   (B) upgrade 更新 will emancipate us
     (C) proposal 提案 from all the hard work.
     (D) impression 印象

142 (A)
所有新員工將會在這個月底 前受到使用新的設備

140. (A) vary = change = alter
C   (B) varies
     (C) varying adj.不同的
     (D) variation 變化
→He never varies his
habits. 他從不改變習慣
That sort of thing
18 varies from person to
person.

142. (A) All personnel will be trained on the new
     equipment by the end of the month
A   (B) Supervisors completed a tour of the
         facilities yesterday
(B)長官昨天完成
3設備,場地(工廠)
參觀
     (C) Unfortunately, the installation fee cost
         more than we had anticipated
(CC)很不幸地,安裝費
比我們預期的要高
     (D) As you are aware, our industry is
         increasingly competitive adj.好競爭的
(CD)如你所知的,意識到的
我們的行業越來越競爭 ɪ e ɪ
competitive advantage 競爭優勢

Questions 143-146 refer to the letter.

OFFICE ORACLE SUPPLY CO.

established 1982 *n. 聖賢哲人, 至理名言*

3589 W. Des Moines Avenue
Des Moines, IA 60034
(404) 243-0924

I'm not an oracle; I don't have a solution to everything.
我不是聖人, 我無法解決所有的問題

October 22
Ms. Clara Helms
World 2 Go Travel
901 W. Harper Street
Cedar Rapids, IA 60034

His teachings were accepted as oracles by the older generation.
老一代的人將他的教導當作聖言

The message was passed by an oracle. 訊息是由傳神諭者傳遞的.

Dear Ms. Helms, *謝謝你不購買我們的ABS塑膠匣（印表機粉）*

Thank you for your purchase of 10 Magenta ABS Plastic Cartridges for CubePro

3D Printers from Office Oracle Supply Co. Your online order was received on

November 1 and is ready for shipping. -------. *11/1收到您的線上訂單, 已經可以運送了*

感謝您向我們訂購辦公室用品 *為了表達感謝, 這筆訂單給您打9折 書記的, 辦事人員的 牧師的*

We appreciate that you have chosen Office Oracle for your company's clerical *神職人員的*

and office needs. As a show of thanks, we are applying a 10 percent discount to

this particular order. Additionally, we are including a reimbursement of shipping charges.

144.   **145.** *除此之外, 還包含了運費的補償（不收運費）*

Enclosed you will find the adjusted invoice and a check for $124.00.

隨函附件您會看到調整過後的收據發票和124元的支票 look forward

Office Oracle is pleased to welcome you to the family and ------- to providing you

*我們公司很榮幸歡迎你加入大家族且期待提供您有品質 **146.***

with quality products and service in the future. *的商品和服務*

Sincerely,   (x)Your sincerely (0) Yours Sincerely
John Stevenson(x)Your's sincerely ✱represent *The dove represent peace.*
Customer Service Representative → *v. 描繪, 聲稱 鴿子象徵和平*

感謝你有興趣應徵我們公司的職位   象徵, 扮演, 演出 He represented the

143. (A) Your interest in employment
        opportunities with us is appreciated
    (B) Unfortunately, we are writing to inform
        you of a delay in delivery *很不幸地, 我們寫來通知你貨運有延遲*
    (C) However, it seems that you have failed
        to reply *但是, 看起來你沒有成功回覆*
    (D) You may expect to receive your order
        in 5-7 days *你將在5-7天內收到訂單的貨品*

144. (A) ongoing *前進的, 不間斷的*
    (B) complimentary *免費的, 贈送的*
    (C) particular
    (D) sequential → *automatic sequential operation 自動連續操作*
        連續的 + follow接順序的文件

145. (A) For example *plan is practical.*
    (B) Still
    (C) However *他聲稱計劃可行.*
    (D) Additionally *adv. 附加地, 同時*

146. (A) leaves room *will provide 90-day*
    (B) looks forward *technical support.*
    (C) goes back
    (D) pushes harder *此外, 公司提供90天技術支援*

adj. 特殊的, 詳細的 獨特的, 挑別的

The witness gave us a particular account of what happened. 解釋說明 目擊者把發生的事詳細說一次

GO ON TO THE NEXT PAGE.

19

*curb
(V)控制,過止 已探取措施 抑制通貨膨脹 (N)控制,抑制,路邊
Measures have been taken to curb inflation. He parked his car to the curb.

Directions: In this part you will read a selection of texts, such as magazine and newspaper articles, e-mails, and instant messages. Each text or set of texts is followed by several questions. Select the best answer for each question and mark the letter (A), (B), (C), or (D) on your answer sheet.

*introduce v.介紹,引見,採用,提出   *refine refined   *deter
v.提煉 adj.精緻的 v.使打消念頭

Questions 147-148 refer to the following article. discourage
The vice chairman of the committee introduce a topic for discussion.
=dissuade

努力 為了抑止民眾不健康的吃飯習慣,丹麥推出新稅/提出議題
試圖 In an effort to curb residents' unhealthy eating habits, Denmark
推出 針對食物的包含超過2.3飽和脂肪
has introduced a new tax on foods that contain more than 2.3 percent
肥胖稅 普遍視為這類稅法是第一個
saturated fat. The "fat tax," generally regarded to be the first of its
將會使食品價格提高 如奶油,牛奶
kind in the world, will raise the prices of foods like butter, milk,
起司 披薩 肉 和油 仍然 有些問題(就是)這個稅是否真的可以
cheese, pizza, meat and oil. Still, some question whether the tax will
打消民眾買商品的念頭 還有其他問題(就是)
actually deter people from buying the products, and others question
如飽和脂肪是否是最需要注意的食物成分 有鑑於
whether saturated fat was the wisest food component to target, given
鹽 糖 和 精緻碳水化合物 也可以被視為對人體有害
that salt, sugar, and refined carbohydrates can also be detrimental to
上 adj.有害的
people's health. Danish officials say they hope the new tax will help =harmful
丹麥政府說希望新稅會幫助限制民眾攝取垃圾食物 但是有些消費者 =hurtful
limit the population's intake of fatty foods. However, some consumers
開始屯貨來打擊(對抗)價格提升 有些生產者說這項稅制很過分
have begun hoarding to beat the price rise, and some producers have
=store 其他人說,像其他丹麥人一樣,已經開始去國外買東西
called the tax an outrage. Others say that they, like many other
e 來避稅了
Danes, have already started shopping abroad to avoid the tax.

outrage 違反   (N)暴了不法行為,侮辱,冒犯,不法行為
(V)激怒,傷害 Such conduct outrages our rules of morality. 這種行為違背我們
肥胖稅是什麼? 哪一項不是肥胖稅的結果?的道德標準

147. What is true about the "fat tax"? apply to
C (A) It applies to all Danish food products. 適用所有丹麥的食品 適用於
(B) It will cause more people to get fat. 會導致更多人變胖
(C) It is probably the first of its kind in the world. 可能是世界上同種類的第一個
(D) It targets the most unhealthy food choices. 他的目標鎖定最不健康的食物

→ cause v.導致,引起,使發生
n.原因,理由,目標

148. Which of the following has not been a result of the "fat tax"?
A (A) Danish citizens have lost more weight. 丹麥民眾少了比較多體重
(B) Producers have complained. 生產者有抱怨
(C) Consumers have begun hoarding supplies. 消費者開始囤貨
(D) Some consumers are altering their shopping habits to avoid the tax. 有些人轉變消費習慣來避稅

You have no cause to complain. 你沒有理由抱怨
World peace is a cause we should all work for.

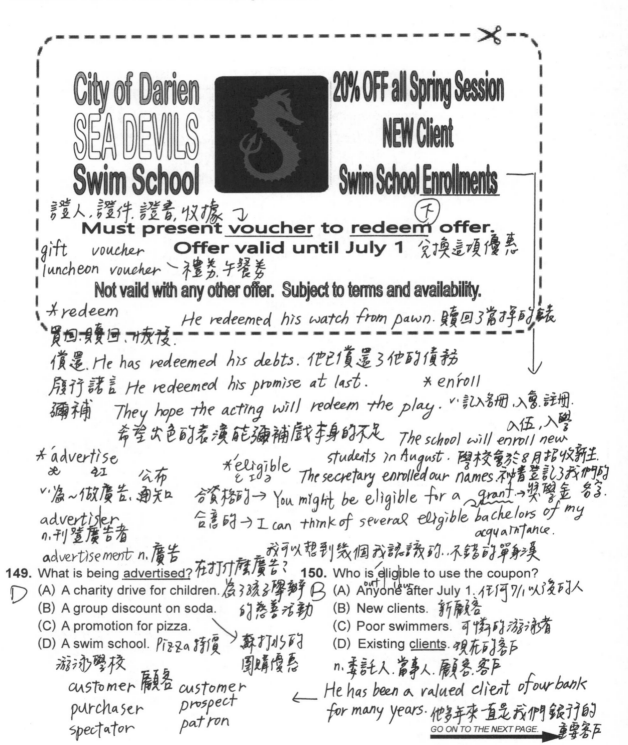

City of Darien SEA DEVILS Swim School

證人,證件,證書,收據

Must present <u>voucher</u> to <u>redeem</u> offer.

gift voucher
luncheon voucher ～禮券,午餐券

Offer valid until July 1 兌換這項優惠

Not vaild with any other offer. Subject to terms and availability.

20% OFF all Spring Session NEW Client Swim School <u>Enrollments</u>

※redeem
買回,贖回,恢復.
He redeemed his watch from pawn. 贖回了當掉的錶

償還. He has redeemed his debts. 他已償還了他的債務

履行諾言 He redeemed his promise at last. ※enroll

彌補 They hope the acting will redeem the play. v.記入名冊,入會,註冊.
希望出色的表演能彌補戲本身的不足 入伍,入學

The school will enroll new students in August. 學校會於8月招收新生.

※advertise
光 虹 公布
v.為~做廣告,通知

The secretary enrolled our names. 秘書登記了我們的名字

※eligible
合資格的→ You might be eligible for a grant. →獎學金 名字.

advertiser
n.刊登廣告者

合意的→ I can think of several eligible bachelors of my acquaintance.

advertisement n.廣告
我可以想到幾個我認識的,不錯的單身漢

149. What is being <u>advertised</u>? 在打什麼廣告?
(A) A charity drive for children. 為了孩子舉辦
(B) A group discount on soda. 的慈善活動
(C) A promotion for pizza.
(D) A swim school. Pizza的特價
游泳學校
customer 顧客
purchaser
spectator
customer
prospect
patron
蘇打水的團購優惠

150. Who is <u>eligible</u> to use the coupon?
(A) Anyone after July 1. 任何7/1以後的人
(B) New clients. 新顧客
(C) Poor swimmers. 可憐的游泳者
(D) Existing <u>clients</u>. 現在的客戶
n.委託人,當事人,顧客,客戶

He has been a valued client of our bank for many years. 他多年來一直是我們銀行的重要客戶

GO ON TO THE NEXT PAGE.

✗ enthusiasm

The proposal was greeted with great enthusiasm.
這個建議受到熱情的響應

(n.) 熱心、熱情、熱忱、愛好
= warmth = passion = optimism
= devotedness = vigour = eagerness
= earnestness
= keenness

to show enthusiasm for sth.
to arouse enthusiasm in sb. about
to arouse sb. to enthusiasm
激發某人的熱情

{gardening is his latest enthusiasm
cooking}
他最近迷上園藝
做飯

✗ showcase
v. 展示、陳列
n. 展示櫃

memo
Memorandum

TO: GTS Sales staff
FROM: Karen Moore
DATE: April 18
SUBJECT: Customer Presentation

你上週準備要展示給客戶看的新產品線演講真是太棒了!

The JSKL Marketing presentation you prepared

last week to showcase our new product line was

exceptional!
展示
= outstanding adj. 傑出的、優秀的

展示優點的地方

✗ strategy
= planning = tactics
戰略、計策
策略、對策

Your enthusiasm, sales strategy and product

knowledge were impressive and certainly sealed

the deal with Mr. Lockhart!
交易釘住 = 交易沒問題、會成功
{seal the deal
break the deal}
agreement

你的熱忱.銷售策略
和商品知識(對商品的了解)
都讓人印象深刻
而且絕對簽下了
和L先生的合約

outstanding
= eminent
= prominent
= distinguished
= significant
= noticeable

Thank you for your outstanding work and dedication.
distribute
Bonus checks will be distributed next week.
away | give   分而之分發

謝謝你超棒的表現
和付出.
紅利支票下周會發出

My sincere congratulations to all of you!
✗ ɔ e
這部劇是顯示劇團優秀水平的嘉現.

The opera is a stunning showcase for the company.

誰會做銷售報告?
151. Who gave the sales presentation?
C (A) Karen Moore.
He is resigned to his fate. 他聽天由命
(B) Mr. Lockhart.
(C) The GTS sales staff.
(D) The JSKL marketing team.

下週會發生什麼事?
152. What will happen next week?
D (A) Mr. Lockhart will visit the office.
(B) Karen Moore will resign. 辭職
(C) JSKL will sign a contract. 簽合約
(D) The GTS sales staff will receive bonus checks. 會收到獎金支票

✗ resign v. 辭職、使聽從、把~託交給
again
The general resigned his commission. 將軍辭去了他的職務
She resigned her children to the care of her sister. 把把孩子交給妹妹照顧

22

Questions 153-154 refer to the following advertisement.

WILD WILLIE'S USED CARS

SPRING BONANZA LIQUIDATION SALE

NO DEPOSIT! NO PAYMENT UNTIL 2019!

THIS IS WILD WILLIE'S CRAZIEST DEAL EVER

- 48 month financing at low rates
- FREE comprehensive mechanical warranty
- FREE Roadside Assistance program

CHECK OUT OUR LATEST ARRIVALS

2013	Mercedes-Benz E650 10K miles, one owner, spotless	15,550
2013	BMW M4 15K miles, convertible, metallic gray	13,330
2014	Lexus L300 7K miles, ABS, GPS, loaded	12,000
2015	Tesla Roadster 10K miles, electric, gas miser	22,000
2015	Mercedes-Benz E180 4.5K miles, factory trade-in	24,440
2016	Porsche 911 Turbo, 2K miles, showroom model, nice!	33,330

153. What is this advertisement for?
(A) Roadside Assistance.
(B) A sale on used cars.
(C) New Cars.
(D) An automotive warranty.

154. Which of the following is NOT offered by the ad?
(A) 48 month financing.
(B) No deposit.
(C) Free warranty.
(D) No payment.

GO ON TO THE NEXT PAGE.

23

Questions 155-157 refer to the following advertisement.

Date posted: June 6   Views: 249   Replies: 198

⭐ $3100/2BR <u>DOWNTOWN</u> OAKLAND APARTMENT FOR RENT — (Lake Merritt BART)

A spacious two-bedroom apartment in the Essex on Lake Merritt will be ready for a new tenant on July 1. It is conveniently located across from the Lake Merritt BART station, giving residents quick access to the San Francisco business district and many other destinations in the Bay Area. It is a leisurely walk to popular nightlife options and dining establishments in the Uptown area. Vacancies in this highly desirable residence are rare. The unit is located on the 18th floor and has a large terrace. Located on a relatively quiet and peaceful street, the Essex soars above the other buildings in the neighborhood, so it is full of natural light as well. The unit has beautiful hardwood flooring and a contemporary kitchen with energy-efficient appliances. One designated parking space in the underground garage is included. The Essex on Lake Merritt residents receive a substantial discount at the Kinetic Fitness Center located in the shopping center adjacent to the building. The apartment will be open for tours this weekend, June 8-10. Rent is $3,100 per month. A one-time deposit of $9,300 is also required. This deposit and the first month's rent are due upon signing of the rental agreement.

To <u>apply</u> please e-mail <u>vacancy@essexproperties.com</u>

155. What is suggested about the apartment?
(A) It was recently remodeled.
(B) It is close to restaurants.
(C) It is on the top floor of the building.
(D) It is fully furnished.

156. What is included with the apartment?
(A) A transit pass.
(B) A cleaning service.
(C) A fitness club membership.
(D) A parking space.

157. What is indicated about the Essex on Lake Merritt?
(A) It is in the center of the business district.
(B) It has several shops in the lobby.
(C) It is taller than the other buildings in the area.
(D) It currently has many unoccupied apartments.

24

INTERNSHIP (PAID)

Recruitment, HR, and Training Support

With 60 restaurants and food service operations on both the East and West Coasts, PRG offers world-class dining experiences. The East Coast corporate office is looking for a bright, energetic individual to support the East Coast HR department.

Responsibilities:
- Supporting the recruitment manager and the recruiting process.
- Working with the Training Manager.
- Managing recruitment, orientation and training materials.
- Drafting, revising and posting job ads on a weekly basis.
- Running errands for the reception desk if needed.

Requirements:
- Currently enrolled or graduated from a hospitality or business school and interested in HR.
- Meticulous attention to detail.
- Solid writing skills and ability to communicate effectively with all levels of management.
- Interest in food a plus
- Strong knowledge of MS Word preferred but not required.

Interested candidates may apply online at: www.PatinaGroup.com

158. Who might be interested in this position?
- (A) Recent college graduates.
- (B) High school students.
- (C) Someone who hates writing.
- (D) Spanish teachers.

159. What is preferred but not required?
- (A) A strong background in the Arts.
- (B) An interest in cooking.
- (C) A strong knowledge of MS Word.
- (D) Experience working with the disabled.

160. Where is this job opening located?
- (A) The West Coast corporate office.
- (B) The East Coast HR department.
- (C) A restaurant on the West Coast.
- (D) A reception desk on the East Coast.

GO ON TO THE NEXT PAGE.

25

Questions 161-163 refer to the following magazine article.

Beneath the world's oceans lie rugged mountains, active volcanoes, vast plateaus and almost bottomless trenches. The deepest ocean trenches could easily swallow up the tallest mountains on land.

Around most continents are shallow seas that cover gently sloping areas called continental shelves. These reach depths of about 650 feet (200 m). The continental shelves end at the steeper continental slopes, which lead down to the deepest parts of the ocean.

Beyond the continental slope is the abyss. The abyss contains plains, long mountain ranges called ocean ridges, isolated mountains called seamounts, and ocean trenches, which are the deepest parts of the oceans. In the centers of some ocean ridges are long rift valleys, where earthquakes and volcanic eruptions are common. Some volcanoes that rise from the ridges appear above the surface as islands.

Other mountain ranges are made up of extinct volcanoes. Some seamounts, called guyots, are extinct volcanoes with flat tops. Scientists think that these underwater mountains were once islands but their tops were worn away by waves.

161. What is this article mainly about?
(A) Mountain ranges.
(B) Earthquakes.
(C) The oceans.
(D) Volcanoes.

162. What are guyots?
(A) Extinct underwater volcanoes.
(B) Long rift valleys.
(C) Active earthquakes.
(D) Continental slopes.

163. What is true about the abyss?
(A) It is located on top of the continental slope.
(B) It contains the deepest parts of the ocean.
(C) It swallows other mountain ranges.
(D) It produces the shallow seas.

26

Baltimore, Maryland, has a very long and rich history. It is perhaps best known for being the site of the historic Battle of Baltimore during the War of 1812. Over the course of the battle, British invaders bombed Fort McHenry with rockets as Francis Scott Key wrote, "The Star-Spangled Banner," which would become the American national anthem. Baltimore was also the site of the first casualty of the American Civil War.

Baltimore also has a large African-American population that has played an important role in its history. African-Americans have had a major presence in Baltimore since the Revolutionary War. During that time, they were brought to Baltimore as slaves from Africa. Baltimore was also one of the hotbeds during the American Civil Rights movement and famous African-Americans such as Thurgood Marshall and Kweisi Mfume have made Baltimore their hometown. R&B artists such as Tupac Shakur, Dru Hill and Mario have also emerged from Baltimore. Currently, African-Americans form a majority (within the city limits) at 64%.

164. According to the report, what is Baltimore best known for?
(A) Barbeque ribs.
(B) R&B music.
(C) Being the site of a historic battle in the War of 1812.
(D) As the hometown of Thurgood Marshall.

165. What famous song was written in Baltimore?
(A) "Ridin' Dirty," by Tupac.
(B) "The Star-Spangled Banner" by Francis Scott Key.
(C) "America, the Beautiful" by Dru Hill.
(D) "Blowin' in the Wind," by Bob Dylan.

166. What is true about African-Americans in Baltimore?
(A) They bombed Fort McHenry.
(B) They started the Civil Rights Movement.
(C) They prefer R&B to all other kinds of music.
(D) They form a majority within the city limits.

167. How long have African-Americans had a major presence in Baltimore?
(A) Since slavery ended in the United States.
(B) Since the War of 1812.
(C) Since the American Revolutionary War.
(D) Since the Civil Rights Movement.

GO ON TO THE NEXT PAGE.

Questions 168-171 refer to the following article.

Economic theory suggests that individuals place some value on their time. When it comes to walking, time to destination can be minimized by walking more quickly. Unlike other possible determinants of preferred walking speed which become less favorable at higher speeds, time to destination becomes more favorable (less time spent walking) with increasing speed. Value of time therefore likely represents a key factor influencing preferred walking speed.

Scientists from Sweden measured preferred walking speeds of urban pedestrians in 31 countries and found that walking speed is positively correlated with the country's per capita GDP and purchasing power parity, as well as with a measure of individualism in the country's society. People living in more affluent places and therefore with higher economic values to their time generally walk more quickly.

This idea is broadly consistent with common intuition. Everyday situations often change the value of time. For example, when walking to catch a bus, arriving marginally after the bus has left may result in a relatively long wait. Here, the value of the one minute immediately before the bus has departed may be worth 30 minutes of time (the time saved not waiting for the next bus). The idea of hurrying to catch a bus has become almost a cliché. Supporting this idea, individuals who are "hurried" under experimental conditions are less likely to stop in response to a distraction and arrive at their destination sooner.

168. What does the article suggest?
(A) People living in more affluent places generally walk more quickly.
(B) Modern walking speed is based on personal preference.
(C) Personal income has no influence on walking speed.
(D) Individualism is the sole determinant for preferred walking speed.

169. What is the article based on?
(A) Urban legend.
(B) Popular opinion.
(C) Common intuition.
(D) Scientific research.

170. What is this article mainly about?
(A) The relationship between walking speed and value of time.
(B) The preferred walking speed of individuals.
(C) The concept of common intuition.
(D) The key factors which determine GDP.

171. Which of the following is NOT a key factor influencing preferred walking speed?
(A) Value of time.
(B) Purchasing power parity.
(C) Individual freedom.
(D) Experimental conditions.

28

Nearly half of China's wealthiest citizens are considering emigrating, with the United States and Canada the most popular destinations, according to a new report from the authors of China's rich list. The survey by the Bank of China and the Hurun Report, which publishes luxury magazines and runs a research institute, found that 46 percent of Chinese with assets worth more than 10 million yuan ($1.6 million) were considering moving abroad. Another 14 percent had already begun the process, it said. Many said they were seeking a better education for their children and cited concerns about the security of their assets in China. Nearly a third of the respondents said they already had investments overseas, in many cases to enable them to emigrate. Some countries offer residency to foreign citizens who are prepared to invest large sums.

High inflation and the difficulty of investing overseas were also cited in the survey, which took in 980 people in 18 Chinese cities. More than 30 years of booming economic growth have allowed some Chinese to build up vast fortunes once unthinkable in the nominally communist nation. China now has 271 dollar billionaires, according to Hurun's 2017 rich list, up from 189 last year, despite the global economic crisis. The latest report said that 960,000 people in China are now worth more than 10 million yuan, up by 9.7 percent from 2016. Many of the country's wealthiest citizens have made their money in China's construction and property sectors, as well as a growing domestic retail market. But the rigid education system, rising living costs and widespread corruption have led many to look for homes abroad.

GO ON TO THE NEXT PAGE.

172. What is this report based on?

(A) Results of a laboratory experiment. 現象，奇蹟

(B) The author's personal opinion.

(C) Classified government documents.

(D) A survey of 980 rich people in China. n. 調查，調查報告，民意調查，概論

survey v. 調查，審視：She serveyed herself in a mirror. 鏡中端詳自己

173. What does the report say?

(A) Corruption in China has led to a widening gap between the rich and poor. widen v. 擴大，放寬，加寬

(B) The Chinese education system is slowly catching up to Western counterparts. 追上，趕上 / 用額外時間做某事（以彌補所耽誤的時間）

(C) Nearly half of China's wealthiest citizens want to live somewhere else. I've got a lot of work to catch up on.

(D) China has more billionaires per capita than any other country in the world. 人均

174. What does the report suggest?

(A) Individual wealth is a relatively new phenomenon in China.

(B) Nobody is safe from the Chinese government. adv. 無限地，極其

(C) Life in the United States is infinitely better than anywhere else in the world. A burst of hand-clapping followed the ending of the song. 響起一陣掌聲

(D) China's real estate bubble will eventually burst. v. 爆炸，爆裂，n. 爆炸，缺口，突發

175. What does the survey say?

(A) Over half of respondents cited education as a reason for wanting to leave. 超過一半的回覆者說教育是想離開的理由

(B) Nearly a third of respondents say they already have investments overseas. 將近 1/3 回覆者說已在海外有投資

(C) The majority of Chinese billionaires made their fortunes the old fashioned way. 大約有一百萬人被認為是

(D) Approximately a million people are now considered dollar millionaires in China. v. 考慮，認為，細想 百萬富翁（美金）

173.
(A) corruption
腐敗，壞，貪汙，賄賂
→ The heat accelerated the corruption of the dead body.
熱加速了屍體的腐壞
大陸的貪汙導致了富人和窮人間的大差距

millionaire 百萬富翁
億萬富翁
遊戲大富翁 monopoly
大躍起的中國
億萬富翁用傳統方式賺錢

(B) 中式教育系統以緩慢的速度追得上西方的相對應之物（西方教育系統）
counterparts 相對應的人和物

(C) 大陸最有錢的民眾中有半都想住在其他的地方

(D) 大陸和世上其他國家比，平均有更多的億萬富翁

172 (A) 實驗室的實驗結果
(B) 作者的個人意見
(C) 分類的政府文件（機密的）
(D) 針對大陸 980 位有錢人的調查

174
(A) 個人的財富在大陸是個相對新的現象
(B) 在陸政之下沒有人是安全的
(C) 在美國的生活一定比世界其他地方來得好
(D) 大陸的房市泡沫化最終會爆發

So many good ideas! It's too *absorb ⑤ 汲取，理解（知識）*
much for me to absorb all at once. ①吸收 *又完全被書吸引，全神貫注在書上*

JACKSON LIGHTING SUPPLY ② 吸引 *He was utterly absorbed in the book.*
1234 First Avenue ③併吞: *Small business are absorbed by big ones.*
Scranton, Pennsylvania ④承受: *she won't be able to*
Phone (234)555-5555 *absorb another heavy*
On the web: http://www.jax.supply.com *blow.* 把 *精力用來承受沉重的打擊*

important *due to 由於 = because of*
Dear Valued Customer,
由於原物料和其它物品的成本抬高，和其他的營運開支，我們很遺憾地要抬高商品的價格
Due to the rise in raw material costs led by fuel and other commodities and
various other operating expenses, we must unfortunately raise the cost of
our products to you. *raise 舉起，抬起，增加，提高，募款 →*
雖然我們已經做了所有努力來避免抬高價格，我們不再能夠吸收所有的增加（成本）
While we have made every effort to avoid raising our prices, we are no
由於這情況特有把售價提到高的增加10% 售價上
longer able to absorb all increases and as such will be applying a price
預言書，我們生意模式 的改變和進行中的
increase of 10% for our products. Please be aware that changes in our
設備投資 和科技投資
business model and on-going investments in equipment and technology
讓我們能提供 商品和條款(狀況)可以支持市場需求(所言市場要的)
have enabled us to provide products and terms that support market
requirements and keep increases to a minimum. 並且把增加保持在最小的狀況
這樣的增加會讓我們持續提供你一直依賴我們給予的完整服務和商品
This increase will allow us to continue to provide you the complete range
of quality products and services you've come to depend on from Jackson
Lighting Supply.
take effect
請查看我們新的價目表，11/1或之後下單的都通用這個價格 生效
Please review our new price list, which takes effect with orders placed on
or after November 1. Also note that any existing orders will be honored at
your current prices. 也請注意，任何現有的訂單將通用現在的價格
我們很感謝你在這艱困時期的持續支持和光顧
We want to thank you for your valued business and continued support
during these difficult times. We really appreciate your understanding
我們很感謝你任的諒解，關於必要增加
regarding the necessity for this price increase. 的價格
n. 需要，必要性 / necessary adj. 必要的
If you have any queries regarding this change then please don't hesitate to
contact me. *honor 承諾，兌付，實踐，使增光*
/ánxɪ/
Sincerely, He honored his promise. 兌現他的承諾
Don Jackson Will you honor me with a visit? 有榮幸能邀請你來嗎?

GO ON TO THE NEXT PAGE.

JACKSON LIGHTING 公司

NEW PRICE LIST AS OF NOVEMBER 1

購買商品項描述 ~~之前的價格~~ 新價格

Item/Description	Previous Price	New Price
Altman 6" Scoop v.規定.指定	12.50	13.75
Altman 6" Fresnel 為~開業方	13.00	14.30
Altman Par 64 → We should all do as the law	9.00	9.90
Altman Par 40 Strip prescribes.	8.00	8.80
MBT Par 36 我們都應依法辦事 3.00		3.30
MBT Par 36 Color Wheel	7.00	7.70
MBT Source → Do not prescribe	11.50	12.65
MBT Iris to me what I'm going	11.50	12.65
ETC 10 Degree to do. 不要規定我	10.00	11.00
ETC 16 Degree 做什麼事.	12.00	13.20
ETC Ellipsoidal → The doctor	22.00	24.20
Philips Par 4/8/16 prescribed three	4.00	4.40
Philips Par 32 days' rest for her.	6.00	6.60
Philips 6" Scoop	11.75	12.92
Philips 6" Fresnel	12.25	13.47
Philips R40 Ellipsoidal	20.00	22.00

prescribe

＊單字補充 transplant

1. 移植.移植: We'll transplant the flowers to the garden.

2. 便移居: Many English people were transplanted to Ireland.

3. 移植: The doctor transplanted skin to her face.

4. 移居: Adults are not flexible; they do not transplant comfortably to another place.

＊transform

1. 改造.改革.改善: The situation has been greatly transformed. 情勢已大為轉

2. 變换.轉換: A tadpole transforms into a frog. 蝌蚪變成青蛙

176. What is the main purpose of the letter?

C

(A) To place an order. 下訂單
(B) To request an action. 要求一個行動
(C) To explain a price increase. 解釋價格增加
(D) To demand a refund. 要求一個退款

↑man
hand

177. What does the author ask the recipient to do? 作者要求接收者做什麼?

D

(A) Reorder their supplies. 重新訂購補給品 C
(B) Change their business model. 改變他們的商業模式
(C) Deliver and install a product.
(D) Contact the author if they have any questions. 若有任何問題請聯繫作者

運送及安裝商品

178. What will happen to existing orders placed before November 1? 目前已存在, 11/1號前的訂單會怎樣?

B

(A) The orders will be cancelled. 會被取消
(B) The orders will be honored at existing prices. 會以現有的價格收費
(C) The orders will be filled by a different company. 訂單內容將會由不同的公司處理
(D) The orders will be processed at the new prices. 訂單將會以新價格處理

179. What does Jackson Lighting Supply most likely sell? 最有可能是在賣什麼的

C

(A) Cameras. 相機
(B) Hand tools. 用于操作的簡易工具
(C) Light bulbs. 燈泡
(D) Party Supplies. v. 供給.供應.提供
派對用品 n. 供給品.庫存

180. James placed an order for 10 Altman Par 40 Strips on October 29. How much did Jackson Lighting Supply charge him? James 在 10/29 下3筆訂單 請問 JLS 公司會收他多少錢?

(A) $30.00.
(B) $33.00.
(C) $80.00. *charge v. 索費.庭攻.控告.充電
(D) $88.00. → He was charged with stealing. 他被控有偷盜的行為

* This is Daisy at HR.

Could / May I speak with/to from Annie, please?

* I'm calling for Annie in Marketing.
Can you please put me through to Annie?

*公司打電話補充

請打我的手機
(X) Please call my cell phone.
(O) Call me on my cell phone.
(O) Call me at this number.

打到我的辦公室
(X) Call me in the office. → 句意模糊, 不知是
(O) Call me at work. 要對方從辦公室打
Should I call you at home 或是打到你辦公室
or at work? 我該打你家裡還是公司?

謝謝拉你的來電
(X) Thank you for your calling. → 謝拉你的召喚
(O) Thank you for your call.
(O) Thank you for calling. → call 變動名詞不是 "calling" <召喚.天職>

* What was his calling? (X) 他在呼喚什麼?
(O) 他是做什麼工作的?

GO ON TO THE NEXT PAGE.

* in the distant past 久遠的過去   in the recent past 不久的過去
                    future 未來   future 未來

Article 1

有跡象顯示全世界都有地球正在暖化的紀錄

Signs that the Earth is warming have been recorded all over the

最容易觀察到增加的溫度就是透過去150年以來的溫度計紀錄

globe. The easiest way to see increasing temperatures is through the

heat 溫度計   n.

thermometer records kept over the past century and a half. Around the

全世界地球的平均溫度上升了華氏1度

world, the Earth's average temperature has risen more than 1 degree

華氏   ℃ 攝氏的過去一世紀以來

Fahrenheit (0.8 degrees Celsius) over the last century, and about twice

在北極的部分地區是兩倍 (上升2度)   *figure out

that in parts of the Arctic.   想出,解出

←→ Antarctic 南極

雖然我們不能看好幾千年以前   但有紀錄可以幫助我們知道當時的久遠很以前

Although we can't look at thermometers going back thousands of

的氣溫和濃度

years, we do have some records that help us figure out what

(溫室氣體濃度)

temperatures and concentrations were like in the distant past. For

例如,樹木儲存了生活地的氣候資訊

example, trees store information about the climate in the place where

每一年,樹長得更粗並形成新的年輪 (annual rings) 在較暖和較潮濕

they live. Each year, trees grow thicker and form new rings. In warmer

年輪會比較粗   老樹和木頭(老木材)可以告訴我們 的年分裡

and wetter years, the rings are thicker. Old trees and wood can tell us

關於幾百甚至幾千年以前的狀況

about conditions hundreds or even several thousands of years ago.

電腦模型幫助科學家理解地球的氣候或是長期的天氣模式.

Computer models help scientists to understand the Earth's climate,

模式   模型也可以讓科學家對於未來氣候做預測)

or long-term weather patterns. Models also allow scientists to make

預測,模擬=simulation   基本上,模型模擬大氣和海洋吸收太陽

predictions about the future climate. Basically, models simulate how

能量然後傳送到整個地球

the atmosphere and oceans absorb energy from the sun and transport

影響太陽能到達地球表面多少的因素就是

it around the globe. Factors that affect the amount of the sun's energy

這些模型裡頭驅使氣候變化的原因

reaching Earth's surface are what drive the climate in these models, as

如同在真實世界裡。 這些因素包含如溫室氣體,大氣裡的粒子

in real life. These include things like greenhouse gases, particles in the

比如像燒火山來的粒子   還有從太陽本身來的能量改變

atmosphere (such as from volcanoes) and changes in energy coming

ㄨ ㄛ ㄟ   ⑦

from the sun itself. And what these computer models are showing is

that the Earth is steadily getting warmer.   (活) active   * dormant

而這些模型顯示出來的是地球正漸的變溫暖 (休) dormant   volcano adj. 休眠的

(死) extinct   靜止的

n. 氣氛: The talk was conducted in a cordial   *extinct adj. 滅絕的

情趣: The ancient place has a lot of   atmosphere.   失效的

魅力   atmosphere. 古老的地方很有魅力.   會談是在熱情友好的

                                            氣圍中進行的.

34

*obvious = manifest adj. 明白的, 清楚的, 顯然的
hand | strike   v. 證明, 實 The speech manifested the truth
                            of the story.

Article 2

很多人說全球暖化很明顯而所有反對的言論都是錯的
Many claim that global warming is obvious and that all arguments

但問題是常常我們眼中"很明顯的"事爭並不總是真實的
against it fail. The problem is that often what is "obvious" isn't always

關於全球暖化的擔憂被誇大了而且誤導了
true. Concern over global warming is overblown and misdirected.
                                              = exaggerated
氣候科學常說電腦模型就是事實
Climate science is often reported as if computer models are facts.

電腦模型無法把理論的真假區分出來,因為並不是測量事實
A computer model can not discriminate theories into true and false

那樣的模型可能可以給出一個在哪裡
because it is not measuring reality. Such models may give one an

實驗的想法,但是聲稱可以證明所有事一定絕對不正確的,而且讓人存考來源的
idea where to experiment, but to claim they "prove" anything is pure

打折(不全信)   準確性.
fiction and should lead one to discount the source. At best you can

                                    最好的情況是你頂多用電腦模型
use a computer model to disprove a theory. 來反駁些理論(但是常是是全對的,不可以)

所有關於地球暖化的預是基於電腦模型
    All predictions of global warming are based on computer models,

而非歷史的資料   而且   衛星   判斷   對流層
not historical data. Furthermore, satellite readings of the troposphere
(也就是科學家說暖化會馬上出現的地方)   a   ʒ   工
(the area where scientists say global warming will immediately

自衛星判讀的23年以來並未發現暖化所跡象
appear) show no warming in the 23 years since these readings

這些判讀精確度在0.01攝氏之內而且和氣象氣球一致
began. These readings are accurate to within 0.01 degrees Celsius,
                                                          只有以陸地為測量
氣球~一致
and are consistent with data from weather balloons. Only land-based

基礎的氣溫站數不出暖化的跡象<   而這些氣象站並沒有
temperature stations show a warming trend, and these stations do

涵蓋整個星球   無法說明附近城市發展而產生的熱氣
not cover the entire planet, do not account for heat generated by

和是人類見不高的易的影響   * planet n.星球
nearby urban development, and are subject to human error.   plant n.植物
大眾需要知道僅用個模型在電腦上   易受~的影響   工廠
    The public needs to recognize that just because something is plate n.盤子

不能對二可以代表真實
modeled on a computer, it does not necessarily represent reality, and

                                            *通常 ment 是 n. 結尾.
the result of bad public policy can be expensive.   ment 是 v. 結底常見的頭

而且不好的公眾政策會帶來昂貴的結果.   compliment n.v. 稱讚

                                            complement n.v. 補充

* accurate = precise 精確的   experiment n.v. 實驗

* consistent with 和~一致
  com | stand

*trend 趨勢 = tendency   * be subject to
           = inclination   易受~的影響

GO ON TO THE NEXT PAGE. ➡

181. In what way do the two articles differ?

A

(A) Opinion. 兩篇在何種方面是不相同的
(B) Length. 長度 → 意見
(C) Vocabulary. 單字
(D) Subject matter. 主題

歷史資料
2篇文章在何種面向是類似的
adj. historical
+ novel

182. In what way are the articles similar?

B

(A) They agree on the subject. 同意主旨
(B) They discuss the same subject. 討論相同
(C) They blame the same person. 主題
(D) Neither is based on fact. → 責怪同個人
2者皆非基於事實

183. According to the first article, what is 地球何者為真?
根據第一篇文章.

B

(A) It is slowly getting colder. 慢慢地變冷
(B) It is steadily getting warmer. 穩定逐步地變暖
(C) It is obviously getting wetter. 明顯地變潮溼了
(D) It is probably getting drier. 可能變得更乾
ㄚㄛㄝ

★ subject 大概,或許
n. 主題.題材 → He will probably refuse
話題 the offer. 他很可能拒絕
學科 English is my favorite subject. 這就
理由 議

adj. 易受~的. 易患~的. 以~為條件的
My mother is very subject to headaches.
我媽很容易頭痛
Japan is subject to earthquakes.
日本常有地震
Our plans are subject to the weather.
我們的計畫取決於天氣如何.

be subject to 受~的控制; 有~傾向
→ This party is subject to government supervision. 這個政黨受政府的監督
→ The country is subject to earth-quakes. 這個國家常鬧地震

184. According to the second article, what are all predictions of global warming based on? 根據文章2. 所有的暖化預測是基於什麼而來的?

C

(A) Historical data. 歷史資料
(B) Tree rings. 年輪
(C) Computer models. 電腦模型
(D) Weather balloons. 氣象氣球

+ record 記載 + background 背景

185. What does the author of the second article imply? 作者2暗指什麼? misinform

D

(A) The general public is misinformed 誤導. about global warming. 全球暖化 向~誤報
(B) Global warming can't be found in tree rings. greenhouse effect 溫室效應
(C) Greenhouse gases have not contributed to global warming.
(D) Global warming might be real but no one can prove it.

↓ v. 證明. 證實. 顯示
The lawyer proved the innocence of her client.

(A) 大眾被誤導了關於全球暖化的事
(B) 全球暖化無法在年輪中發現
(C) 溫室氣體不能導致全球暖化
(D) 全球暖化可能是真的但是無人能夠證明

★ contribute to
捐助. 促成. 幫助
How much did you contribute to the fund?

Your suggestion has greatly contributed to the accomplishment of our work.

*Captivate v. 迷惑 (把心抓住) → The children were captivated by her story.
孩子被她的故事吸引住

MILTON BRADLEY THEATRE SET TO REOPEN

在幾10年的開創性表演. 吸引觀眾之後
MB劇院非常需要一頓整修

SPRINGFIELD, MA (April 8)—After many decades of groundbreaking performances and captivated audiences, the Milton Bradley Theatre was in great need of refurbishing.

椅子的靠墊已更換. 現在靠塗外面
是葡萄酒色的布料
而大廳的概念台和陽台的概念台 (販賣部)

Designed by Werner Royitz in a post-modern style, the building was visually stunning when the theatre first opened, but it had begun to show its age. Although the theatre had retained its beauty over time, it was in need of some care to ensure that this beauty would endure into the future.

由WR設計的後現代主義風格
這棟時初剛開幕
時視覺上非常震撼
但已經開始顯視出年分歲
能夠捕捉過這些時間
仍保有它的美麗
已仍需要一些的照料來維保
它的美能夠延續到未來
I could endure it no longer. 我無法再忍受

After an extensive renovation, the theatre has reopened. The grand chandelier and impressive murals in the lobby have been thoroughly cleaned, the seat cushions have been replaced and are now covered in a burgundy fabric, and the concession stands in the main lobby and on the balcony floor have been enlarged and remodeled. In addition, a new parking garage, the final part of the renovation project, is expected to be completed in September.

在大規模的輕修之後
劇院重新開幕. 大廳主要的大吊燈
和令人印象深刻的壁飾
也被增大和重新輕修過了
除此之外
新的停車場
整修專案的最後一個部分
預計在9月時完工

The reopening coincides with the 30th anniversary of the theatre's resident company, the Milton Bradley Players, whose next play is the world premiere of *The Last Centurion* by renowned playwright Benjamin Glass. The show will be directed by the theatre's own artistic director, Ocasio Del Potre.

劇院的重新開幕和劇院的當地企業30周年時間 一致
n. 周年紀念 adj. 週年的. 週年紀念的
下一部劇是世界首演的 "最後的百人隊長"
是由著名的劇作家
BG寫的
這部劇將由劇院自己的
藝術指導ODP
來導演
adj. 藝術的. 精美的. 精彩的

by J. David Cromm

* stunning
= attractive = dazzling
= gorgeous = amazing
= ravishing = astonishing
= glorious = surprising
= astounding

* concession
together | yield
→ The matter was settled because they made mature
→ At last, their company obtained the mining concessions.
最後. 他們得到了採礦權
→ a refreshment concession 營業權. 營業場所
租地設小吃攤的營業權
concession:
特許權

GO ON TO THE NEXT PAGE.

A FRIENDLY REMINDER FOR THEATRE PATRONS

Please turn off all electronic devices before the performance begins.

You are cordially invited to join us for an informal question-and-answer session with the director and cast immediately following the show. In honor of our 30th anniversary, we are offering audience members a chance to win a free complimentary pass for two for next year's entire season!

This opportunity is _available_ during all performances of _The Last Centurion_ (April 18-May 15). Simply complete the form on page 27 of this program, tear it off, and place it in the box in the lobby during _intermission_ or at the end of the show. A winner will be _selected_ _at random_ on May 15 and contacted by e-mail.

From:	Kristen Lawler <kLawler@funtech.com>
To:	Don Weinstein <dweinstein@mbtheater.com>
Re:	Congratulations! You're the Winner!
Date:	May 18

Dear Mr. Weinstein,

Thank you! It's such a wonderful feeling to have won a free season pass for two for the next season. For your information, I have attended dozens of shows at the Milton Bradley Theatre that I have enjoyed very much. I was particularly impressed by _cast_ of _The Last Centurion_, and the Q&A session was _exceptionally_ _informative_.

Needless to say, I am _looking forward to_ using my season pass.

Thank you so much!

Sincerely,

Kristen Lawler

38

186. What is a purpose of the article? ⓥ 向~誰致詞 對~說話

A

(A) To announce the reopening of a theater. 宣布戲院重新開幕 稱呼

(B) To review a theater company's recent performances. 看戲院公司最近的表演

(C) To report changes to a theater's upcoming season. 報導戲院即將來到的表演季 的改變

(D) To invite the public to a theater's anniversary party.

邀請大眾來戲院的年度派隊

187. According to the article, what is 根據文章 9月什麼 scheduled to be ready in September? 會好?

A

(A) A parking lot. Ⓕ

(B) An adaptation of a play. 一部劇的改編

(C) An expanded snack bar. 拓寬的點心吧

(D) An education center. 教育中心

根據戲院節目表廣告,民眾如何能參加比賽?

188. According to the theater program insert, ＊insert how can people enter the contest? n. 插入物

C

(A) By e-mail. Submit 提交·使服從
 使屈服

(B) By mailing a submission to the theater. 郵寄申請書

(C) By depositing a form in the lobby.

(D) By visiting the theater's website.

把表格放在大廳 去戲院的網頁

＊deposit

v. 放·寄存·儲存·沉積

He deposited 5,000 dollars in the bank.
You can deposit your bags at the counter.
The river deposited silt at its mouth. 河口沉積淤泥

＊adaptation n. 適應·改編
 apt adj. 適合的
adapt v. 使適合·改編
adaptable adj. 能適應的
→ The soil is adaptable to the growth of peanuts.

189. Who will address audience questions after the performance? 表演之後

D

(A) J. David Cromm. 誰會回應聽眾

(B) Werner Rovitz. 的問題?

(C) Benjamin Glass.

(D) Ocasio Del Potre.

關於 L小姐敘述何者為真?

190. What is suggested about Ms. Lawler?

B

(A) She met Mr. Weinstein at an event in April. 4月活動見過面

(B) She attended a performance of The Last Centurion. 參加曬讀

(C) She has ordered a ticket subscription for the next season. Ⓕ

(D) She organized the question-and-answer session.

她負責Q&A環節

她已訂了下一季的票

書中插頁·夾著的散頁廣告

v. 插入·刊登

→ They inserted an advertisement in the newspaper. 報紙上刊登一則廣告

→ The book would be improved by inserting another chapter.

這本書如果再插入一個章節就更好了

→ She inserted a patch in the sleeve.

他給袖子打了個補丁·

inapt adj. 不適宜的
aptitude n. 才能

→ He has no aptitude for this work.

＊subscription n.

subscribe v. 捐款·訂購·同意·簽字
under｜write

→ He did not subscribe to my proposal.

GO ON TO THE NEXT PAGE.

Questions 191-195 refer to following online message board, e-mail, and webpage.

*appreciate → I'm afraid you haven't appreciated the urgency of the matter. → Her talent for music was not appreciated.

欣賞 感激 領會   我怕你沒有理解事情的緊急性   沒人欣賞他的音樂才能

TEPHRA.com

www.tephra.com/forums_t/radio/mix103

Welcome to Tephra 火山碎屑
Join. Start. Engage.

REGISTER NOW

告知,通知 → He advertised them of his decision to withdraw from the election.
①.為~做廣告;為~宣傳 ② 他告知他們他要退出選舉的決定

137
Has anyone advertised with Mix 103? (self.tephra)

Submitted August 13 by **Suzanne Harris** 有人和Mix103合作過登廣告嗎？
有沒有人有和Mix103廣告部門接觸的經驗嗎?任何回應都感謝.

Does anybody have any experience dealing with the advertising
deal with 處理
department at Mix 103? Any feedback would be greatly appreciated.

*significant
adj.重大的,顯著的,意義深長的

Submitted August 15 by **George Swinney**

我有從3月開始在 Mix102 Radio 登廣告,事實證明是個聰明的選擇
I have had advertisements running on Mix 103 Radio since last March. It
最近幾個月,我看到了來店客人數目的大幅成長
has proved to be a smart choice. In recent months I have seen a significant
increase in the number of customers visiting my business, Imbur Interiors.
很多人跟我說是聽了電台廣告才來的   (店的名稱)
Many tell me it was the radio advertisement that brought them in.
當我和電台簽約時,有些非預期的收費產生,但O小姐,廣告部門的,把我的
When I signed a contract with the station, there was a problem with some
非預期中的
unexpected charges. However, Ms. O'Meara from the advertising
把憂慮轉達給她上司,而問題很快就解決了
division section department brought my concerns to her supervisor, and the matter was
一週過後 O小姐甚至回電給我
quickly resolved. Ms. O'Meara even checked back with me a week later to
assure ensure I was pleased with the outcome. *matter n.事情
guarantee 確保我對於簽約的結果滿意   ② 物質: Matter exists in
three status: solid, liquid and gas.

v.要緊 It doesn't matter.   物質以三種形態存在,固,液,氣
*concern   ③事態: to make matters worse
n.關心的事   (複數) There's nothing we can do to change matters.
That's no concern of mine. ② 涉及,使擔心 = He is concerned for her safety.
不關我的事   He was very concerned about her.
40

From:	Casey O'Meara
To:	All Staff
Re:	Final Broadcast
Date:	September 29

*intern n. intern 實習生，實習醫生.
v. intern 拘留，軟禁
*draw v. 畫，描畫，拉，拔，取出，提錢，吸引.
n. 拉，抽，平局 The game ended in a draw. 平局結束

因為我的實習要結束了，希望你們知道我在這裡工作是個很愉快的經驗。我很感激在這裡得到的訓練和建議，在過去這12個月以來

Dear All,

As my internship at Mix 103 Radio draws to a close, please know
that working here has been a wonderful experience for me. I am
= marvelous = remarkable = extraordinary

grateful for the training and advice I have received over the past
twelve months.
*fundamental 基礎的 The fundamental cause of his success
n. 基本原則，法則 adj. 根本的 is his hard work.

我特別想感謝我的老闆兼指導老師(教導他的人) Leslie. 從他身上我不僅
I'd especially like to thank my boss and mentor, Leslie Brighton, from
學到廣播廣告的基礎
whom I have not only learned the fundamentals of radio advertising,
同時也達到客戶的需求
but also how to meet customers' needs. Her nomination for this
name n. 提名 nominate v. 提名

year's Orlando Trophy speaks volumes about her dedication to her
clients and staff. 他被提名今年的 Orlando Trophy 表代著他對客戶和員工的大量貢獻

我也很感激你給我看的影片錄影，給我看在這裡的工作和娛樂
I also appreciate the video recording you presented to me, showing
我會想念和你們很多人一起在 Michele Pizza
me at work and at play here. I will miss joining many of you for
吃午餐 我知道你們全部的人有我的聯絡資訊
lunches at the Michele's Pizza. I know that all of you have my
keep in touch *dedicate
contact information, so don't hesitate to stay in touch! d e
正式午餐 luncheon 不要猶豫和我保持聯絡吧! (v.) 以～奉獻，把(時間 精力)用於
Sincerely, 舉行落成典禮
*subscribe
Casey O'Meara 捐款: They subscribed to local charities.
*前3句是已認識了 訂閱，訂購: He subscribed to Orlando Business Today.
保持聯繫 認購 : Each of us subscribed for 350 shares.
第4句則是開始聯繫 同意 : He did not subscribe to my proposal.

1. Keep in touch. ⟷ We didn't keep/stay in touch.
2. Stay in touch. ⟷ We lost touch. 你抵達時請聯絡我
3. Be in touch. 4. Get in touch with me when you arrive.

GO ON TO THE NEXT PAGE.

*recipient ⓝ 受領者；接受者；容器 They would in time become the recipients of
Orlando Small Business Trophy Winners 小企業冠軍得獎者 much criticism.
最終會受到許多批評

Advertising and **Social Media** Category 廣告和社群媒體類

白金獎 platinum + handshake 將大筆遣散金(遣散費) + disc 白金唱片

Platinum: Leslie Brighton, Advertising, Mix 103 Radio *trophy sized + fish (adj)
金 client 接受的
Gold: Nina Li, Marketing, Davenport Clothing Stores 幾乎可以去比賽的戰利品 能接受的
銀
Silver: Jorge Cortez, Cortez Publicity Company
銅
Bronze: Thom Royce, Social Media Technology, Mix 103 Radio

得獎者是從50位提名者中選出來的   白金獎的得獎者將會在
Winners were selected from over 50 nominations. The recipient of the
12月出刊的 今日奧蘭多商業中被介紹
Platinum Orlando Trophy will be profiled in the December issue of Orlando
Business Today. Awards will be presented by the Orlando Business n. 出刊物，爭論，爭議
3 He died without
Association (at a gala event (in the banquet hall (of the Peachtree Disney   issue.
Hotel (on October 12. 獎項將會在10月12號，Disney飯店，宴會廳舉辦的慶祝活動中
由OBA頒發。[用介系詞拆句子，由後往前翻譯]

*gala n. 盛會，節目，慶祝   *adequate adj. 足夠的，勝任的 He proved adequate
*profile v. 概述，描述，畫   ə ɔ ɪ   適當的   to the job.

---

191. What does Mr. Swinney indicate about
A   Mix 103 Radio? 為何地解決了他的 問題
解決 (A) It resolved his problem adequately.
=solve (B) It is a rapidly growing company. 迅速成長的
   (C) It advertises local business only. 只打當地商家
   (D) It charges an extra fee to new 新客戶要收費
        clients. 的廣告

她為何寄出這封信件？
193. Why did Ms. O'Meara send the e-mail?
D   (A) To ask for help from co-workers. 向同事求助
   (B) To organize a luncheon. 安排商業午餐
   (C) To arrange a video recording
        session. 安排錄影活動
   (D) To thank staff members. 感謝員工

全體工作人員 幕僚 楊杖 The old man walked with
194. What award will be presented to Ms. a wooden
A   O'Meara's supervisor? staff.
   (A) Platinum. 會頒什麼獎項給他上司？
   (B) Gold.
   (C) Silver. *supervisor
   (D) Bronze. 100人
        mess supervisor 食堂管理員
        board of supervisors 監查委員會

192. What is suggested about Mr. Swinney?
B   (A) He has been a client of Mix 103 他是103的客戶很多年了
        Radio for many years.
   (B) He was assisted by an intern at
        Mix 103 Radio. 103有實習生幫助他
   (C) He recently experienced a decline
        in his car sales. 他最近車子賣不好 =sink
   (D) He runs the biggest automotive =fall
        business in the area. =weaken
他在這區營運最大的汽車生意

195. What does the webpage suggest?
C   (A) The gala event is open to the
        public. 慶祝活動有開放給大眾
   (B) Fewer awards nominations were
        received this year. 今年收到的提名很少
   (C) Mr. Royce and Ms. Brighton are
        colleagues. 他們是同事
   (D) Winners will receive a free
        subscription to Orlando Business
        Today. 得獎者可以收到免費的訂閱
subscribe v. 簽名，署名，認購，贊許
under write 認捐，捐助，同意
(前 頁下)

42

*authorize
v. 授權給, 批准認可, 允許   → A senior member of the commitee was authorized to
→ authorization   act for the chairman during his absence.
n. 授權, 批准   諦不在時, 一位資深的委員被授權代理他的職務.

MEMO

全職的員工要繳交請假表格到公司的"計時"網頁.
當時期被同意後, 通常的長官人員會透過"計時"寄出一封批准信.

To: All Full-Time Staff
Subject: Vacation Days

*appropriate adj. 適當的, 恰當的, 相稱的 → She picked up a dress appropriate for the occasion.

All full-time staff members must <u>submit</u> requests for leave through
the company's Timekeeper website. An <u>authorization</u> e-mail will *approve 贊成批准認可
be sent through Timekeeper (after dates are <u>approved</u>) by the → The government
<u>appropriate</u> supervisor. ↔ 淡季 low season / off-season   has now approved the scheme
外燴服務部門員工: 旺季時要請假(6-9月)需要總經理的額外同意 for the erection of a new public library.
<u>Catering Services Department employees</u>: Note that requests for
vacation during our <u>peak season</u> (June through September) require
additional <u>approval</u> from the <u>General Manager</u>.
peak time 尖峰時間   同意建造新的公眾圖書館

approve v. → n. 認可, 同意, 批准 The plane had the approval of the school authorities.

Supervisors will coordinate with other members of the department
to <u>ensure</u> that all the absent employee's <u>duties</u> will be covered and
will <u>inform</u> the Human Resources team how responsibilities have
been reassigned.   duty n. 職務, 職責 = task, work, assignment, obligation
長官將會和部門的其他人協調來確保所有不在的員工職務
補人做, 並且通知人資那些工作職責是如何被指派的. → 繳交, 屈從 She refused to submit to his control.
Requests for <u>time off</u> should be <u>submitted</u> at least three weeks <u>in</u>
<u>advance</u>. Human Resources will post a calendar on Timekeeper 月曆, 日程表 assign 施配, 分派
with all planned vacations, including names of employees <u>assigned</u> = daybook = log
to cover those on vacation. 休假要求至少要先3週前要繳交. 人資會放行事曆在
"計時"網頁上, 包含所有的人員休假計畫, 包括了被指派要職務代理的人員名稱.
For questions <u>regarding</u> this <u>policy</u>, please contact our Human
Resources Department. *in advance → The guard of honor marched
關於
*policy n. 政策, 方針, 手段   在前面, 事先   in advance. 儀隊走在前面.
Carl Steinberg, Manager
→ He paid a month's rent in advance.
*inform   Honesty is the best
v. 通知, 告知, 告發   誠實是上策   policy. 支付了一個月的房租
He informed her he was thinking of entering medical school.
He informed against the drug pusher. 他告發了那個毒販.
                    drug dealer

GO ON TO THE NEXT PAGE.

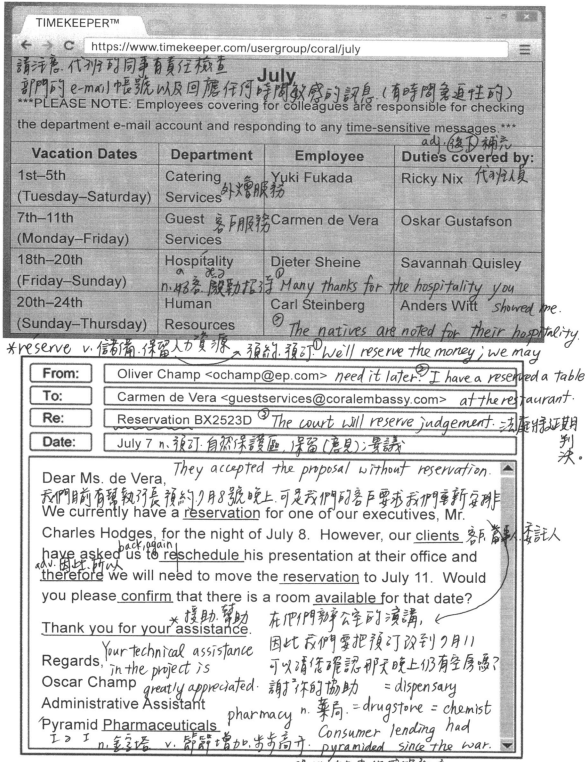

TIMEKEEPER™

https://www.timekeeper.com/usergroup/coral/july

請注意. 代班的同事有責任檢查
部門的 e-mail 帳號以及回應任何時間敏感的訊息.(有時間急迫性的)

PLEASE NOTE: Employees covering for colleagues are responsible for checking the department e-mail account and responding to any time-sensitive messages.

adj. (後項)補充

July

Vacation Dates	Department	Employee	Duties covered by:
1st–5th (Tuesday–Saturday)	Catering Services 外燴服務	Yuki Fukada	Ricky Nix 代班人員
7th–11th (Monday–Friday)	Guest 客戶服務 Services	Carmen de Vera	Oskar Gustafson
18th–20th (Friday–Sunday)	Hospitality n.好客 殷勤招待	Dieter Sheine	Savannah Quisley
20th–24th (Sunday–Thursday)	Human Resources 人力資源	Carl Steinberg	Anders Witt

Many thanks for the hospitality you showed me.
② The natives are noted for their hospitality.

*reserve v. 儲備. 保留. 預約. 預訂 ① We'll reserve the money; we may need it later. ② I have a reserved a table at the restaurant. ③ The court will reserve judgement. 法庭將延期判決.
n. 預訂. 自然保護區. 保留(意見);異議

From: Oliver Champ <ochamp@ep.com>
To: Carmen de Vera <guestservices@coralembassy.com>
Re: Reservation BX2523D
Date: July 7

They accepted the proposal without reservation.

Dear Ms. de Vera,

我們目前有替執行長預約 7月8號晚上. 可是我們的客戶要求我們重新安排

We currently have a reservation for one of our executives, Mr. Charles Hodges, for the night of July 8. However, our clients 客戶. 當事人. 委託人 have asked us to reschedule his presentation at their office and therefore we will need to move the reservation to July 11. Would you please confirm that there is a room available for that date?

back, again
adv. 因此. 所以

Thank you for your assistance. *援助. 幫助

在他們辦公室的演講,
因此我們要把預訂改到 7月11
可以請您確認那天晚上仍有空房嗎?

Regards,
Your technical assistance in the project is greatly appreciated.

Oscar Champ
Administrative Assistant
Pyramid Pharmaceuticals
Ⅰ⊃Ⅰ n.金字塔 v. 節節增加. 步步高升

謝謝你的協助 = dispensary
pharmacy n. 藥局 = drugstore = chemist
Consumer lending had pyramided since the war.
戰後消費者借貸節節升高

44

196. According to the memo, what should an employee do to schedule a vacation? 員工想安排休假該怎麼做呢?

B

(A) Send an e-mail to a manager. 寄email給經理

(B) Visit a company website. 去公司網站

(C) Contact Human Resources. 要聯絡人資

(D) Inform a supervisor. 通知主管

197. In the e-mail, what type of business is Mr. Champ contacting?

A

(A) A hotel. 飯店

(B) A restaurant. 餐廳

(C) An airline. 航空公司

(D) A conference center. 會議中心

198. Who will most likely respond to Mr. Champ's e-mail? 誰會回覆他的信件?

D

(A) Ms. Steinberg. respond ① 回應 ② 回覆 ③ 飯應

(B) Mr. Nix. The patient is responding well to treatment.

(C) Ms. De Vera.

(D) Mr. Gustafson.

＊ lap v. ① 重疊：He lapped one plate over another.
② 包裹：She lapped my finger.
③ 比~領先一圈 By the end of the race Bob had lapped Jihney.
④ 跑完一圈：He lapped in two minutes.
⑤ 舔：The dog lapped up the water.
⑥ 海浪輕拍：Waves lapped against the boat.
n. 舔/一次的分量
— With one lap of his tongue the bear finished the honey.

＊general adj. 一般的·普通的 This is a general magazine.
全體的·公眾的 That is a matter of general anxiety.
籠統的 We had a general talk about drama. 沒討論·沒有很專精

199. Which vacation period in the table will require approval by the general manager? 總經理

C

(A) July 18-20. general public 公眾

(B) July 7-11. ⑦

(C) July 1-5.

(D) July 20-24.

看間表中,關於員工的公司何者為真?

200. In the table, what is indicated about the employees' company? 一週營業7天

A

(A) It operates seven days a week.

(B) It plans to hire additional staff in July 7月可能僱用更多的員工

(C) It requires vacations not to overlap.

(D) It closes some departments in July.

要求假期不能重疊

overlap

② 有相同之處

His interests overlap with mine to a large extent.

他的興趣和我的興趣在很大程度上是相同的

Stop! This is the end of the test. If you finish before time is called, you may go back to Parts 5, 6, and 7 and check your work.

＊sensitive
adj. 敏感的·易受傷害的 → Tina is sensitive to strong smells. 對強烈氣味敏感
易怒的·神經過敏的 → He is sensitive about the failure. 提到他的失敗很易生氣
機密的·過敏的 → It's a sensitive issue. 敏感的問題
→ The child is sensitive to eggs. 對難蛋過敏

GO ON TO THE NEXT PAGE.